Mr Happy And The Hammer Of God & Other Stories

About the Author
Martin Egblewogbe

Martin Egblewogbe was born in Ghana in 1975. He has a BS.c and M.Phil in Physics and is currently working on his Ph.D at the University of Ghana, Legon where he is a Lecturer in the Department of Physics. He enjoys writing short stories and poetry in his spare time and has contributed to several anthologies some of which have been published online, in anthologies and in newspapers including *Look Where You Have Gone and Sit* co-edited with Laban Carrick Hill (Woeli, Ghana: 2011). He is the co-founder and a Director of the Writers Project of Ghana. He also currently hosts the weekly radio show, 'Writers Project' on CitiFM in Accra, Ghana where he lives with his wife and daughter. His hobbies include Still Photography and Astronomy.

Praise for *Mr Happy*...

Martin Egblewogbe's short stories are different from any other stories I have read in terms of content and presentation. This wonderful collection deeply explores the mind and the metaphysical with such a passion and intensity that many other storytellers lack.
Nana Fredua-Agyeman
Image Nations Blog Ghana

Mr Happy And The Hammer Of God & Other Stories

Martin Egblewogbe

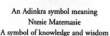

An Adinkra symbol meaning
Ntesie Matemasie
A symbol of knowledge and wisdom

Copyright © 2012 Ayebia Clarke Publishing Limited
Mr Happy And The Hammer Of God & Other Stories by Martin Egblewogbe

My Happy... was self-published in Ghana by Martin Egblewogbe in 2008

This edition is first published in 2012 by Ayebia Clarke Publishing Ltd
Ayebia Clarke Publishing Limited
7 Syringa Walk
Banbury
Oxfordshire
OX16 1FR
UK
www.ayebia.co.uk

ISBN 978-0-9569307-1-2

Distributed outside Africa, Europe and the United Kingdom
And exclusively in the USA by
Lynne Rienner Publishers, Inc
1800 30th Street, Suite 314
Boulder, CO 80301
USA
www.rienner.com

Distributed in Africa, Europe and the UK by TURNAROUND Publisher Services
at www.turnaround-uk.com

British Library Cataloguing-in-Publication Data
Cover Design by Claire Gaukrodger at Oxford
Typeset by FiSH Books, Enfield, Middlesex, UK.
Printed and bound by CPI Group (UK) Ltd, Croydon, CR0 4YY

Available from www.ayebia.co.uk or email info@ayebia.co.uk
Distributed in Africa, Europe, UK by TURNAROUND at
www.turnaround-uk.com

Distributed in Southern Africa by Book Promotions (PTY) Cape Town
A subsidiary of Jonathan Ball Publishers in South Africa.
For orders contact: orders@bookpro.co.za

The Publisher acknowledge the support of Arts Council SE Funding

And it was liberty to stride
Along my cell from side to side
And up and down, and then athwart
And tread it over every part
And round the pillars one by one
Returning where my walk began.
                    –Lord Byron, 'The Prisoner of Chillon'.

Contents

Acknowledgements

Many people have supported my writing in diverse ways. I mention here a few to whom I am much obliged: Kofi Awoonor and the late Su-Tung Wen for their suggestions about Jjork; Mercy Ananeh-Frempong for reviewing *Mr Happy And The Hammer Of God* and *Three Conservations with Ayuba;* and Beth Webb, who reviewed *Three Conversations With Ayuba, Small Changes Within The Dynamic* and *Pharmaceutical Intervention* under the British Council's *Crossing Borders Programme.* Thanks also to Franka Andoh and Norman Ohler for comments on *Mr Happy And The Hammer Of God* and *Coffee At The Hilltop Café* (respectively); and to Andrew Etwire, on whose computer I typed the earlier stories and who partly financed the printing of the first edition.

Martin Egblewogbe
March, 2012.

PART I

They Call Am 'Lie Lie Fight'

Chapter 1

To-morrow

HE WALKED OUT of the office. The sun was shining strongly, a white hot spot that no one could abide at one. It was break time. He would not go back. Maybe he was mad. He did not care. His suit made sense in the air-conditioned trap of the office – in the exploding heat of the tropical outdoors it was insane. He kept the jacket on. His armpits became soaked. Sweat streamed into his eyes and made him squint. The powder was in his pocket. His destination was sure. The beachfront! The bar! Just as for regular lunch – only a little late this time.

The Universe had had enough of man already. An avenue with a verdant green beyond the trees that would bring joy. This was distress – this blistering land-scape with motors and people rushing about raising dust and fumes and noise, only to retire when the sun died and to resume again to-morrow. This was a desperate situation.

But he would go back to work to-morrow. The clients would wait till to-morrow. The world would go on. The sun would come up. The radio would come alive. People would rush to and fro. Life will happen and history would repeat itself.

3

The dustbin of history empties into the landfill of to-morrow, he thought. Nonsense exists in the way we juggle words.

The end was coming. Islam was the religion of peace and the believers emphasised this with blood. There would be rivers of blood as the Jihad came around.

Jesus was also coming. Everybody had had enough. The African gods had long retired to sterile spacescapes in the cold reaches of the Cosmos.

Man was now alone, left to his nefarious devices.

To-morrow he would make all his apologies and ask for forgiveness. Remorseful, he would turn over a new leaf. He would pay his taxes. Everything to-morrow: when the sun came up again the world would be brand-new.

He now understood that society detested the recluse. As he became detached from it all, the only thing he wanted was more silence. Yet when he stopped speaking to people they considered it a hostile act, but how could keeping your peace be a hostile act?

Burdened, weary, the soul was fatigued and maybe it was all because of the abandoned cross. Come to me. *Ecce Homo.*

Somewhere in his mind a woman was weeping. It could not be his wife. He had not asked for a divorce. And he was not dead yet.

He did not care about his wife, not lately at least. In any case it was all a lost cause, this human experiment. His wife – she was impossible to fathom and she cried and she cared about the good life and security. He cared about absolute truth and philosophy. Maybe he had been lucky anyway, marrying her. What if she had turned out to be one of those far out types – the hardened, non-menstruating she-men with muscles instead of breasts, who read Law and spoke in public with much passion and no sense. But those types never married. So his wife could not have been such.

Dreamy sex-starved Freud had a finger on the pulse of humanity.

Women wanted to be like men. Men wanted to be like god.

He wanted the stars. To see the god who made man.

There was noise in the air. On the radio, the TV. In the newspapers. A concatenation of the usual fare. He had heard it all, over and over and over again. War! Victory! Defeat! Cancer! Pain! Love! Resurrection! Dead people arising at spiritual command, to the dismay of the heirs.

The bar! The beachfront! They passed him a dog-eared menu. A list of drinks, not recommended during working hours. An indulgence to be kept secret from the underwriters. He chose a liquid of great strength, whose alcohol content stood cheekily close to the half-past mark.

The refreshment was served, blood-red and glowing maliciously in a tall glass, with a dash of ice.

His fingers passed lightly over the health warning. Cigarette smoke is bad for you but good for the economy. But he did not light up. He wanted to smoke something else, something ultimate. A powerful drug that would make him grin endlessly. He wanted to make love, but not to an ordinary woman – a woman astonishingly lithe and beautiful, with tremendous hips and formidable breasts.

But such were not available.

He pushed the packet away, watching it slide across the table top.

The story had appeared in many versions. There were many forms of the same. The world had run out of ideas, the old templates were used over and over again.

He eased the powder into the drink. It was a sleeping concoction of the old-fashioned kind, in a powder, meant to kill. There was no way he could survive this. He drank steadily; everything down to the dregs.

The stars were glimmering in the sky. He could not remember having seen this earlier.

Chapter 2

Coffee At The Hilltop Café

THEY ARE SITTING just by the window inside the café and she is happily conversing with the man. I can see the two of them quite well through the large glass window; she is laughing heartily at some joke from her partner. Her lovely laugh – I imagine I can hear it now, peals like jewels falling from her lips...

I am seated outside in one of the chairs placed here for those who wish to enjoy the picturesque and refreshing view: the café is near the crest of the hill.

I try not to watch the woman all the time, concentrating instead on my cup of coffee and the view. The coffee is good and strong: the café has a tradition for excellence.

My chair is just a few feet from the street. There is a jewellery shop directly opposite the café; adjacent to it is a beauty parlour and next to the beauty parlour is a tailor's shop. The shops and houses that line the street are painted sedate and stately shades of orange, green and white; their glass windows glint in the late afternoon sun and each entrance looks as inviting as the other. It is a shopping street, but, being late afternoon on a Sunday, is quiet and deserted.

Further off in the distance I can see the mountain peaks against the slowly darkening sky.

Every Sunday afternoon at four-thirty I set off from my house and take a walk up the hill; I get to the Hilltop Café at about five o'clock and order a cup of coffee. Over the next fifteen minutes, I allow myself to enjoy the coffee and the scenery. When I finish my cup, I set off again, down the other side of the hill. Another fifteen minutes brings me to church in time for the evening service.

Today I was saddened, on taking my first sip, to glimpse at the couple inside the café. My afternoon was nearly spoiled, but I quietly drank my coffee, determined not to disturb my afternoon leisure.

So I share my glances between the street and the inside of the café and soon it is all the same to me, whether she is there, or whether she is not there: I enjoy my afternoon cup nearly as much as I have always done.

My fifteen minutes are up; I drain my cup and get up to leave. Inside the café the woman is listening intently to the man, she is looking him in the eye. I cannot tell for sure if the couple inside the café saw me, but it did not seem as if they did.

I reach the crest of the hill just in time to see the sun set.

This evening's display is unusually brilliant. The whole western horizon is tainted a mellow, mature purple, with the sun, a purple-gold orb, sinking majestically behind the tree-crowned hills. The town is bathed in gentle light and wrapped in beautiful shadows. There is perfect

8

stillness and even the gulls winging across the western horizon do not flap their wings, but sail majestically across the darkening sky.

I stop in mid-stride and the beauty makes my head spin. I stand and watch, but the glorious sight soon fades and darkness begins to take over as the sun disappears behind the hills.

I resume my walk. I know I will be in time for the church programme. The street lamps come on, casting a dreamy brilliance onto the street. I think about the girl in the café. It seems that my Sunday afternoon has been spoiled. I'll never go that way again on my Sunday stroll, never pause at the Hilltop Café for my cup of coffee.

I try to enjoy the rest of my walk in the deepening dark. A few people pass me by and I nod quietly in response to their greetings.

I have reached the chapel. This evening an evangelist from another town will conduct the service and the faithful prayerfully await its commencement. The organ is playing softly and the music swells gently in the background.

When I am seated I call to mind the wonderful sunset that I witnessed. It was a fitting epilogue to my long-established habit of a Sunday afternoon stroll with a coffee break. There is something at least to smile about.

I open my Bible but I do not read. I close my eyes and listen to the music. It is beautiful.

Chapter 3

Pharmaceutical Intervention

A CARELESS INCIDENT when under the influence...

The result was bothersome; it seemed to harm the psyche continuously with an interminable vision of an iron vice slowly closing in. In the end, it was not worth all the trouble. It did not help to know that under other circumstances this outcome would have been welcomed gleefully: a good bargain leaves everyone happy.

And everyday, it grew a little.

It was in this relentlessness that the increasing sense of unease lay. Rain or shine, day or night, it seemed unstoppable in its doggedness, though the effect often seemed so innocuous as to be ignorable: just a slight darkening of the nipples, a heaviness in the breasts, an extra line on the test strip. Most prominent amongst the signs was the cessation of the monthly event, yet it almost passed unnoticed. Usually considered an inconvenient routine, a person could almost be glad to be free. Except that the absence meant something else: a clot steadily thickening, thickening at an astonishing speed.

And everyday the anguish of knowledge and the vision

of the vice and the urgency of decision; everyday with stealth towards the day it could not be hid.

So every day...

For many reasons it seemed inappropriate to continue in the present state, though there were warm, cuddly thoughts of a cot and hope of life after life. The moral argument was strong, but so was the social argument; each side fully represented by the habit and the parish. Yet Christ, crossing all crises, was to be listened to above all else. But, could one sin be greater than another, two sins greater than one; were there sins too great to be forgiven.

Everyday, it grew a little.

***

Frantic efforts were made. Someone, moving in clandestine circles, scribbled a name on a scrap of paper. It was restricted, but one could only try. An acceptably seedy pharmacy shop tucked away in a despondent and poverty-ridden neighbourhood was found, chosen because it seemed likely that there, such requests would neither be unusual nor unexpected.

A thin film of dust over the shelf of medicine bottles and boxes was the world of the sick, were there so many ills? A false smile hid the darkness within and the scrap of paper was duly presented. From the Queen of this medicine-demesne there was no smile, only a lens-mediated look of pity from the other side of the counter. Her tired voice, cheerless and aloof, was designed for the dispensation of good sense and medication.

'Some women think that this medication can be used to abort a pregnancy, which is not in fact the case.'

A correct choice of words is much to be desired. What was sought was 'a pharmaceutical intervention to cause a reversion to the former state.' With delicacy, some forms of distress can be avoided. In making the request, therefore, the words were carefully selected, weighed and practised. No allusion was made to illegal purpose.

There are difficulties in the present condition. It is imperative that this mistake be corrected early and more unpleasantness avoided later.

The lexical accuracy of the word 'mistake' could be questioned. Great lies are often hidden in misnomers.

A response required measured tones, normally used for delivering the catechism:

'It was recommended.'

And the reply came in the same polite tenor.

'Still, a prescription is required.'

'At this time I have no prescription.'

'Then, it cannot be sold.'

'It is much needed, I assure you.'

'Nevertheless, the Law must not be broken. A prescription is required.'

Further pleading would tear apart the smooth veneer and expose the growing desperation; perhaps it would achieve nothing else. It was clear that in the openness of the pharmacy shop, even accepting to commit an indiscretion would be hard to do, no matter how cogent the persuasion – and certainly the Queen was not brazen. Thus, slow about-face and exit, poker face hiding sinking feeling. But a small distance away from the shop, discreet whispers came from an alley.

'It is possible to secure the medication at extra cost.'

Would this be the rope dropped to rescue the imperilled climber scrabbling at an impervious rock face, or the rope callously handed to the willing suicide. The offer of salvation could be misleading. Not saved from what, but, saved for what?

The offer was take-it-or-leave-it.

'A special case may be made for your situation. Even so, avoiding the prescription will mean paying more.'

Did the price really matter, when the thing grew even as the voices passed back and forth? The exchange was made, Cash for the Chemical, pressed into pills.

***

There is much wood in the world. Shelves in the pharmacy became trees along the way to a door, opening to a room with a table inside. The cross on the wall hung a Wooden Christ looking on while the chemical was taken as indicated, but with a quickly swallowed shot of absinthe to assist the process. It had been suggested that a little alcohol would only help. The changes were

hormonal; thus, a certain gaiety was noticed. Gaiety, not relief. It was the chemical: the chemical and the alcohol.

Everything living dissolves into blood. However, one is unsure of a decomposing cadaver: there perhaps, blood might be absent.

With the blood came relief and stronger remorse. Absorbent material was at hand; it now helped to put to bed as well. The intervention had been successful, but the problem and its resolution presented remarkably similar mental torment: the vice did not disappear; only the jaws stopped closing. Certain stains are permanent, though concealed within the folds of the garment.

Now the icon of the Holy Mother held greater meaning, the thorns about the Sacred Heart had deeper significance. Each struck a profound and bitter resonance.

And when drowsy, voices crossed over from the other side.

Has it now come to this?

Yes.

The cuddly suckling lullabies of the future. . .

No more.

Murder. . .

But that is certainly extreme. The notion must be rejected.

Evil.´. .

Somehow, its applicability is doubtful.

Sinner. . .

Once again – but perhaps it is not exactly something new, not this far into the journey.

Drowsiness often gave way to sleep. Sometimes, though, there would be an interregnum and a momentary reversion to wakefulness.

Chapter 4

Down Wind

'FROM MY KNEES downwards,' he said into the mouthpiece. 'I climbed up ten flights of stairs, each flight containing ten steps; a hundred steps in all. Then I climbed down again and I felt this throbbing pain in my legs.'

He looked out of the telephone booth. He couldn't see much, because it was raining heavily and it was early evening.

'A deluge, Doctor.' He muttered. 'A veritable deluge.' It had been raining steadily for hours. Doubtless there would be flooding somewhere in the metropolis. Thunder rumbled and a gust of wind blew rain through the crack left by the door, which would not close properly.

'Very uncomfortable in here, Doctor.' The man said. He was not bothered that there was no sound from the other end. He knew that the Doctor was there, patiently listening, or even now quietly making an accurate diagnosis of the problem, prior to giving an appropriate prescription.

'It is a dull pain, but persistent. It begins just from my

kneecaps and continues to the ankle: and yes, it includes the ankle joint.'

Of course the Doctor was listening.

Inside the booth, the window was misted over and rivulets of water coursed down the outside. The man reached out and wiped the cold glass.

A car was driving away. The red taillights shimmered in the rain and the reflection off the wet road shimmered even more. Along the street, two rows of ugly two-storey buildings reared up; here and there a blurred yellow glow indicated the presence of a window.

The man said into the telephone, 'Kind of melancholy, the view from here.'

Surely, the Doctor was listening.

'I did no other exercise, just climbed up to the top storey and spoke to someone. I did not sit down. Then I climbed down. But in the foyer I felt this pain. Suddenly, it was upon me. Certainly you hear me, you understand what I am saying.'

But of course, the Doctor always heard.

'From my knees downward, you see and nowhere else. Otherwise I feel in the best of health.'

But the Doctor would know best, what the pain was symptomatic of.

He thought about how the telephone turned his voice into an electric current and transported it down the line, all the way to some exchange, perhaps to yet another, then onward to the Doctor's telephone scores of kilometres away, which instrument turned the electric current into sound, so that the Doctor could hear him say, 'Maybe I should give you time with the diagnosis, a day perhaps, then I shall call again and you can tell me what is causing this pain.'

He did not feel rude hanging up on the Doctor; it was in the scheme of things. The Doctor did not wish to speak immediately, so it was in order.

The streets were quiet. Rain came down in torrents. Suddenly, the place lit up with a savage flash of lightning and the subsequent thunder clap rocked the booth.

The man wanted to listen to music – a song to go with the wet, soggy evening, as the leaden skies let go of their charge. Blues, by Nat King Cole, or Louis Armstrong perhaps. Or maybe a strange, slow song by Nina Simone. He dialled another number. The response was immediate and curt.

'Yes?'

The man in the booth mentioned his name.

'Oh, you.' There was disgust in the voice at the other end of the line.

'I just called to find out how you are,' the man began.

'Do you think I do not know,' the voice said. 'You cannot lie to me. I know all about it. It was posted on the notice board this morning.'

'Know?' the man asked. 'Know about what?'

'Don't deny it! You cannot deny it. It was on the notice board, behind the glass pane. That you could do something like that!'

'But I have done nothing at all,' he said.

'You lie. It was on the notice board and I'm sure it's still there.'

The man looked out at the rain. It showed no sign of letting up. He did not understand what the other man was talking about.

'What exactly did the notice say?'

'Exactly what you did, you sick fellow.'

'And what did I do?'

'You know best. Perhaps, what was posted did not even report your action in enough detail?'

The man in the booth was a little surprised. What on earth could the other man be talking about? After a brief pause he decided to change the subject.

'How are you?' He asked.

'Very fine, sod you and you?'

'There is no cause for abuse,' he said gently, adding, 'It is raining quite heavily.'

'Here, too. Will you hang up, or should I?'

'No, wait a second. Did you know that...'

There was a click and it was clear that the man at the other end of the line had set down his handset with some violence.

Well, said the man in the booth.

It had become darker. He sought a tune to sing, in keeping with the melancholy air that hung about him. Ray Charles: *Georgia On my Mind*. Gladys Knight: *Midnight Train to Georgia*. There was something about Georgia, he thought.

An especially violent gust of wind sprayed much rain into the booth. The man's shoes were wet and inside the shoes his feet were wet too. Furthermore, there was a pain in his legs, from the knees downward.

A poem, instead of a song, maybe, he mused.

But he knew no poetry.

He said aloud, 'I have to read that notice, posted on the notice board, with something about me in it. Maybe to-morrow, when the rain has let up.'

He dialled another number. As soon as the connection was made he spoke, taking the onslaught this time.

'Do you know,' he began, 'that I am stuck in a telephone booth because it is raining heavily outside. And do you know, that inside the booth there is a smell.'

The voice at the other side asked, 'Who is this, please?'

He did not respond to the query, but went on, 'Now this smell, it is a bad smell. It was in the booth before I came into it. The user before me did well to fill the booth with noisome effluvia from his nether end. But it is raining and I have to keep the door shut. So the smell is trapped inside the booth and so am I.'

There was laughter at the other end of the line.

'Who is this? Do I know you?'

'Of course you do. We know each other quite well.'

'Aha. I thought I recognised the voice. Is this Peter?'

'No, it is not Peter.'

'Or is it Nana?'

'No, it is not Nana.'

'Then who is it?'

'I wish to enquire of you, whether you have seen the notice board.'

'Notice board? What notice board?'

'It is behind a glass pane.'

'What are you talking about?'

'A notice board. Have you seen it?'

'No.'

'It is raining heavily,' the man in the booth observed.

'Look, who is this?'

'It is a terrible smell, I assure you.'

'Hello?'

'Yes?'

'Don't forget to fart before leaving the booth.' Then the connection was broken and he stood listening to the consistent and irritating beeping – a strange electronic sound that had no natural analogue.

But how uncouth.

Maybe I should call the Doctor again, the man in the booth thought, moving his toes inside his wet shoes. But he decided against it. It is too soon, he said to himself; the venerable Doctor is old and slow, even though he is very good.

He did not wish to leave the shelter of the telephone booth and walk through the rain to the bus stop. So he called up another person. This time he introduced himself and described the rainy scene outside to the other person. The man at the other end listened attentively, saying, 'I see' and 'Ha' intermittently. The man in the booth concluded his description in a sad voice, saying, 'I feel sorry for myself.'

'Me, too,' said the other.

'You feel sorry for yourself?'

'No, I feel sorry for you.'

The man was taken aback. He did not see any reason why someone else would feel sorry for him.

'Why?' he asked.

'I do not know. But I'm in my house. It is warm inside and secure. There is music playing on the radio. Real good music. I had to get out of bed to answer the 'phone. Do you know who is there?'

'Who is where?'

'In the bed.'

'No.'

'A woman. A naked woman. Not dead, but alive. Do you understand?'

'Yes.'

The man desperately wanted to speak about the notice that said things about him. He asked, 'By the way, have you seen the notice board?'

'I feel sorry for you. Really I do.'

'There is a notice ... about me ... no don't hang up ...'

Then there was only the hiss of a closed line and it seemed that the telephone itself had given a last gasp and died.

I am wet, the man said to himself. I feel a pain in my legs, from the knees downward. I am trapped in a telephone booth, breathing someone's flatulence. Sometimes the rain blows into the booth. When it thunders violently, the booth shakes. It is fearful when lightning tears up the night. And the noise of the rain, falling, falling, falling onto the booth and making a loud drumming noise.

Outside a car sped by and the headlamps swept through the booth, making the man squint. I should get out of here, said the man. Out, out and home. But it is raining and doubtless I will get quite wet. Besides I might have to wait a while before the bus comes by. The bus, spewing warm bluish exhaust fumes. It will be warm inside, with people inside, going home. Possibly it is illegal to take shelter in a telephone booth. Public property. I am the public. I am a member of the public. I will leave as soon as someone else comes.

The man wondered how long he could remain in the booth, all things considered. 'Not long, not long after this,' he muttered.

He called up a Lawyer he knew and said to him; 'I have received intelligence that information concerning me has been published.'

'What type of information and where was it published?' the Lawyer asked.

'Information concerning certain actions I supposedly carried out. The mode of publication was by notice board.'

'Ah yes: the notice. I have also seen it and I think you will need my assistance.'

The man became afraid. If he would need the assistance of a Lawyer then the issue was serious.

'What did the notice say?' he asked.

'Just that you did it and it said how you did it.'

'Did what? What does it say I did?'

'But you should know what you did.'

The man muttered something about the rain.

'What was that?' the Lawyer asked.

'This is a grave matter,' the man said.

'And I heartily concur,' the Lawyer agreed, adding, 'No one would have thought you could do something like that.'

This is maddening, thought the man in the booth. What on earth did the notice say that he had done?

'This may be slander, you know,' he said to the Lawyer.

'Perhaps,' said the Lawyer, 'and perhaps not.'

The man closed his eyes and listened awhile to the rain.

'What exactly did the notice say?' he asked.

The Lawyer said nothing. The man in the booth remembered the Doctor and his silence over the telephone. Could that have been an expression of outrage? But how could it be? The whole thing had to be a joke.

He said,

'I have done nothing unlawful, neither have I done anything extraordinary. However, there is a pain in my legs, from my knees down. Also, there is a bad smell in the telephone booth, because someone farted into it.'

The Lawyer was silent. The man said, with sudden force:

'Please get a pencil and a sheet of paper.'

'I always have writing material beside my telephone,' the Lawyer replied.

'Very well. I want you to make the following amendments to my Will. If I should die to-night, every garment upon my body and my shoes as well, should be thoroughly cleaned, disinfected and given to the blind man who plays his guitar in front of the General Post Office.'

'You do not have a Will made with me,' said the Lawyer drily. 'How can you amend it?'

'Make a Will for me then.'

'It requires that you come to my chambers to-morrow morning...'

'No!' the man in the booth interrupted sharply. 'I want it now!'

There was rising anger in the Lawyer's voice.

'Listen here. I have no time to be playing infantile games. If you have anything important to discuss, come and see me to-morrow. Good-bye.'

The man in the booth broke the connection quickly, because he wanted to hang up before the Lawyer did. He placed another call. The telephone rang hollowly several times.

'Pick it up you fool!' he shouted. But the connection had just been made.

'What was that?' a tired voice came over the line.

'Nothing... Hello.'

'I heard something, I'm sure.'

'The line must be bad.'

'Never been clearer.'

'Must be the rain.'

'Ah yes, the rain. Look, sir, how may I help you?'

'I wish to speak with you.'

'Aha?'

'I just want someone to talk to.'

'What about?'

'And I want someone to talk to me', the man in the booth said, thinking, How interesting, this conversation. He believed that it held great prospects.

'Of course by now you have seen the notice board,' he began.

'I've seen hundreds of notice boards.'

'This one has a glass pane in front.'

'Scores of them are like that.'

'There's a notice on it about me.'

'So what?'

'It talks about something that I'm alleged to have done.'

'And what did you do?'

'That is what I cannot fathom. I have done nothing untoward or extraordinary, to warrant a notice being put up about me.'

After this there was a long silence. The man in the booth did not mind the wait. But suddenly there came a yell down the line:

'Put it down you fool!'

His heart jumped.

'What was that?' he asked, breathing deeply to keep steady.

'Must be the rain,' came the smug reply.

'No ... I think not.'

'Probably static on the line.'

'But I don't think so ...'

'Listen, you boring, boorish waste of time: I do not want to continue this conversation. Goodbye.'

No one hung up.

'I said goodbye!' the voice was almost a scream.

'I think that you are mad,' the man in the booth said sadly.

'Goodbye! Bye-bye!' the man at the other end was screaming.

Yet neither hung up.

'Goodbye, now. You hear me? Goodbye.'

'Yes, goodbye,' said the man in the booth.

And still no one hung up. In a little while the man in the booth heard sobbing over the line. He said nothing, just looked out of the booth. It was very dark now and the only illumination came from the lights of the houses beside the road. Inside the booth there was no light at all.

He listened to the man crying over the telephone, his sobs punctuated by whispers of 'Goodbye, please...I hope you've finished...bye-bye...why are you doing this to me...hang up please...'

It is a hard life, the man in the booth thought. He said, 'It must be the rain, don't you think?'

But then he noticed that the rain was letting up. The raindrops no longer drummed ferociously against the booth, but had reduced to a soft murmur.

'However, it seems to be stopping.' But the connection had finally been broken. Not by the other, though: the man in the booth had run out of call time. He sighed, hung up and extracted the used telephone card from the payphone. Then he pushed the door open. Fresh, cool wind gushed in, along with a fine drizzle.

'Oh my legs,' he said, standing at the entrance and looking out at the street.

'But the smell is gone,' he added, smiling to himself as he stepped out into the drizzle. He thrust his hands deep into his trouser pockets and hunched his shoulders. He tried to remember a song about rain.

There were no street lamps; the street was lit in patches by light from nearby buildings. Behind him the telephone booth stood, yellow, solitary, dark and deserted: a strange aural terminal to the rest of the world.

Chapter 5

Small Changes Within
The Dynamic

THE BOOT, DISPLACED from the shoe rack, tells a story beyond mere carelessness.

Through the window blinds the vermilion glow of the setting sun filters weakly into the room. Usually the promise of a pleasant nightfall would have been enough to draw me to the balcony; but today, I am looking at the boot.

The story of the boot is told in the silent pictures on the video screen. This is a moment of crisis, yet dimly I can see the glimmer of liberation springing from its resolution.

There is a bottle of whiskey on the table, opened but not poured. I grip the empty glass fiercely and my thoughts struggle to find a way through this maze of fury.

The boot tells a story of a crooked path that should have been left that way. All my life I have always tried to straighten crooked paths, but that has been of no benefit.

Now on the screen, the moment of the boot: the burly man steps back, pushing against the rack with his naked haunches; shoes spill to the ground.

They had tried putting things back in order, but the boot had fallen a little way under the bed and had been forgotten. Actually, this had to do with the angle of vision. I had positioned the camera rather cleverly and I can see more than they could.

Unconsciously I raise the empty glass to my lips; my lips smack at air. I am glad that I have not poured the drink, because I need to think.

Night has fallen.

The video clip has also ended; the screen now stares back a blank blue. The shaded lamp in the corner casts a yellow glow onto the vanity magazines my wife has left scattered about the bed.

My cell phone buzzes: it is my wife. Bitterness rises within me like cold bile up my throat. I grit my teeth until the little machine falls silent, its colour screen dimming slowly like the reproachful shutting of an eye.

Then the telephone on the bedside table begins to ring: shrill, insistent beeps pulsating with a note of urgency. I press the speaker button.

'Fidelia,' My voice is taut.

'You are ignoring me,' my wife says, pausing slightly before adding: 'I have been delayed at the hairdresser's.'

Her voice is lovely. This is one of the reasons why it is impossible to have a shouting match with her; she keeps her tone gentle even when saying the most abominable things. I always sound unreasonable whenever I shout at her.

I resist an urge to mention that my boot is lying under the bed.

'I shall be home in half an hour.' She says.

So why did she call? To find out where I am.

'Why aren't you talking to me?'

I stare glumly at the blue screen.

'I know that you do not care about me.' She sounds sulky.

Altogether I care too much.

'Forty-five minutes, alright? That should be seven-ish,' she says.

'In that case, I shall still be awake.' I reply.

Another slight pause.

'Yes,' she says.

I hang up.

Life has not been fair to me. I've always thought of myself as a survivor, a man who always manages to beat the odds, but today I see the full extent of my losses – I have been deceived, deceived...!

Of course, the boot has a lot to do with it.

Still, a pyrrhic victory can be won. My salvation now lies in pulling something back from the abyss, something to soothe my wounded pride.

I stroke the button on the remote control and the video clip begins to roll again. In accordance with Fidelia's expensive tastes the entertainment unit is extravagant.

There had been whispers before my wedding, painful, snide murmurs that drifted to my hearing. *Who is that woman? Is this his best shot? Oh, now he's marrying a whore. After all these years, only to end up with...* I bore the insults stoically, but I was just being a fool.

And yet if I had married her because I wanted to be a rebel, I would be worthy of forgiveness. But it was not rebellion. It was weakness and the weak take a beating. God made it so. Let the weak say they are strong. Else they get whipped. Foolishness and weakness cannot be forgiven.

After just a few months, it was clear that I had ended up in an awful predicament. Fidelia was not what I had hoped she would be: popular advice usually has some value.

She was a thorn in my flesh, always telling me about her past sexual escapades and brushing aside my feeble protests. She thinks that I am benefiting from her long experience.

Don't lie, dude; I know my way about the sheets and your orgasms prove it.

On a bad day she would tell me many stories. She knew I cringed. Maybe she did it to punish me. But punish me...for what?

George, remember I told you about George – he had the BMW convertible. He was the first to take me like that. I loved it from the first.

Lord, What am I doing with a woman like this?

Kofi was tipsy, so I drove the car to Fred's place. Kofi urged me to stay over. Maybe they had planned it beforehand...

Her favourite topic was her frolics with Kofi and Fred, which she found greatly amusing.

How could she expect me to love her, when she said all these things?

Then I realised that my wife was seeing other people.

34

She did not care about me; she only wanted my money – and my vows have kept me bound.

Divorce would only be an admission of my error; public derision would be unbearable. Besides, her reaction to a divorce would be awful. Fidelia could be mean and petty and vicious – certainly there would be damage. Terrible damage.

Maybe I should be more reasonable: half-a-loaf and a bird-in-the-hand and all that.

But all this is feeble-mindedness!

The miniature digital video camera, if well positioned, provides a wide-angle view. It has a motion detector and can be programmed to start and stop automatically. Certainly, the manufacturer deserves credit: apart from some blurring and the occasional flicker, the picture is clear and the images distinct. All features can be distinguished: the activities recorded are unmistakable.

Fidelia in coitus with a man. In my bed, on my couch and shamelessly in vehicles.

It is an understatement to say that the scenes are disturbing. The kaleidoscope, a riot of unruly colours shifting this way and that, has suddenly shattered to reveal a terrible, painful reality.

Now is the moment for strength.

I am going to kill her.

And suddenly I breathe easily; the fire in my mind abates. Adrenaline surges through my veins. At last, I am a real human being.

Doubtless this reaction is due to a malformed, malfunctioning psychology: a repressed ogre rising from

35

beyond the fancy terms to deliver a terrible mental blow in real life. Yet only because I am a man, who perhaps has gained the whole world and lost his soul.

Now I will snatch my soul from the devouring fires: I will be free.

Fidelia. Picture-perfect, lust-inspiring belle. My wife.

Replay.

Oh the misery technology can bring: on the glowing screen it is worse than I could ever have imagined. How could she?

The bitch!

I am going to kill her.

Only this thought is able to quell the erupting bitterness within and keep me sane. I will exact retribution for all my failures with women, which have culminated in this abysmal marriage.

Yes.

Even if I do not meet her standards, I am still a man, with hot blood in my veins.

I could dispose of the body; remove incriminating evidence. The builders have just begun putting up my new house – Fidelia could disappear into the foundations and rest in peace under the concrete floor.

A cover-up is possible but unnecessary, because I do not care what happens after she is dead. The important thing is that my spirit will be free the moment I exact retribution for this crowning humiliation. These are magnificent, cosmic concepts – not petty, trite things about adultery or dead love.

This is about liberation.

At seven o'clock the door will open. She will come in. The end game will begin.

I shall strangle her. A gun would be too... remote, a knife too bloody, a cudgel too clumsy. With my hands there will be intimacy. I will stroke her and kiss her and lure her into thinking I still love her... gently I will grab her throat and squeeze... She gasps and fights for breath, but still I squeeze... She claws and kicks at me but I press harder... Then the light is dying in her eyes and I whisper why I have to keep my grip until her pretty head falls limp on my shoulder. . .

I will do it with these very hands that make the money she spends. That would be cathartic, which, in the end, is what I seek – compensation and catharsis. A payback.

The front door opens with a squeak; there are footsteps in the hallway. Stilettos, announcing her presence: she is early by fifteen minutes. It is not my intention to have the video playing when she enters, but it does not seem a bad idea at all.

In horrible expectation, I watch the bedroom door swing open smoothly.

It is all very ordinary. One would have expected otherwise: a portentous creak, perhaps, or a momentary difficulty in opening.

Two people step in. Fidelia, my wife and the man whose sex I have been watching on video. Of course, I have to be impressed at her audacity. Bringing the man into my bedroom! In my presence! Fidelia flashes a disarming smile at me and says:

'Hello my dear, this is Mike.'

What does this woman *really* want with me?

The cloying smell of her perfume makes me think of a funeral parlour and, looking at her long, silky black hair falling in an alluring sheen over her shoulders, I feel only a steel resolve within my being.

I will kill two people instead of one. I have become strong and evil: power surges up my spine as I reach for my briefcase, where my arsenal of self-defence – a loaded .22 – lies concealed.

The video screen finally catches Fidelia's attention. She gasps and clutches Mike's shoulder, pointing at the flickering obscenities. Mike considers the pictures with a slight frown, as if he is just mildly irritated. He turns to my wife.

'Told you the man was plotting something.' The guttural voice is in stark contrast to Fidelia's smooth, gentle tone. 'Damn right you were,' she replies.

Mike reaches out and squeezes her waist.

'You must trust me.' His tone is grim.

My blood is boiling: there is a tightness across my forehead and I must kill him now. I flick the briefcase open. The .22 is in a holster strapped to one side.

'You had no right.' Fidelia says, fixing me with a stern glance before turning back to the screen. 'That was an invasion of my privacy.'

But she seems pleased with the pictures: her eyes widen at a naughty antic.

'Oh Mike...! You were so bad...!' she laughs.

This is the final straw. Anger pounds my brain like killer waves lashing a foundering ship; yet inside I am crying as I reach for my gun.

Mike, however, is not watching the screen.
He is pointing a huge automatic pistol at me.
God is on the side of the big guns.
Fidelia will get everything; I have not made a will.
That cylinder on the snout is a silencer.
I look at the boot.

Chapter 6

———————

Spiral

CERTAINLY THERE WAS some profound meaning in all this. There was purpose; there was a plan. Effort must have been put in to make all this happen. It couldn't all have happened by chance, that certainly would be the wildest and most unreasonable explanation of all. And yet that would be the easiest explanation of all, that everything was by chance. For if it was not by chance then who, what, where, when and why?

But if it was all by chance then there was no profound meaning, only a profound pattern.

A hiss and a loud 'ping!' announced the arrival of breakfast, in the manner in which all his meals were delivered from below. It made no sense if the victuals came from above. But from how far below he could not tell.

With another 'ping' a little metal door in the wall slid open and a loaded dinner tray lay revealed on a stainless steel platform. It was a small elevator system: after the meal was over he would return the dishes and the tray to the platform. The little metal door would slide shut.

Sometimes he toyed with the idea of escape via that

route, but the space was only large enough to carry the dishes and the occasional bottle of wine. In any case the mechanism was such that the elevator did not operate until the door was shut and therefore it was impossible to escape by first inserting part of his body – his feet perhaps – and when the platform started down, by pushing the rest of his body into the increasing space. However, he made no attempt to escape. He was fully convinced that such an action would be futile.

The dining table in the cell was not large. It was meant for two people and had a round formica top with a most exquisite design: startling white, with an ingrained spiral of vanishing grey. The spiral started out in the middle of the circular top and spread out in tight windings to the edge. The table legs, made of stainless steel, were just about as thin as his little finger and each was coiled into a helix.

There were two identical chairs at opposite sides of the table, made of polished wood and steel.

At every meal he wondered about the other seat, standing mockingly vacant. He liked to think that the chair stood expectant of some great happening. And what was a more natural expectation that the chair would at a point in time have an occupant?

He had never sat in the other chair, preferring always to sit facing the stout metal grille that was the entrance to his cell. The door was a solid affair and fitted snugly into the archway of the entrance. The vertical bars had only enough space between them to allow his hand through. Beyond the entrance he could see the steps that led up to the cell. They came from below, but only the first few steps were visible: the rest bent out of sight. He knew that it was a spiral staircase, extending all the way down. Through the bars he also saw the steps as they led up from the door, again bending out of sight. This fact bothered him immensely, because it indicated that there could be some destination above him that was worth going to. He did not mind so much if the stairs passed other places before reaching his cell.

Sometimes he pressed his face against the cold metal bars of the door, trying to see more than met the eye, but the narrow stairwell and bare stone wall revealed nothing.

After breakfast he set the tray back into the elevator and as the door shut and the dishes were whisked away, he walked to the single window at the other side of the cell. There was a wooden stool beside the window. The stool had only one leg – a slender affair that split into five branches at the base with a castor at the end of each branch. The stool moved easily on the castors and it was a great comfort to sit on.

He looked out of the window. To his left were mountains, the peaks rearing insolently upwards, in mute challenge to his cell and to the skies. To his right the mountains fell steeply to a wooded forest, presenting such a great expanse of foliage that he wondered which was more majestic: the cowing brutishness of the rocky masses, or the endless expanse of the forest.

The bars in the window were set wider apart than the bars in the door. He put his head through the bars and looking down, it appeared that the tower rose from nothing. Yet that could not be the case, he mused. It was only that the distance to the ground was so great that his eyes failed him. For there had to be a ground – if there was no ground, there would be philosophical difficulties. Then he looked up, squinting from the glare. The tower extended a great distance upwards as well and he could not tell where it ended. From the sides he saw that the tower had rounded edges. The tower was a vertical cylinder of great length.

At the end of the cell opposite the elevator door there was a bed, standing close to the floor and bearing a marvellously soft mattress. A little way beyond the foot of the bed was an oval bath tub made of white marble and served by two taps – one delivering hot water and the other delivering cold water. There was a water closet also, squat and sturdy. It was rather noisy when flushed and the man often wondered at the thought of his excreta constrained to move within a pipe, thundering through the great distance all the way down, at a terrible speed perhaps. It made sense that his excreta should return to the source of his food, that way the cycle would be complete: an open cycle was intolerable even to think about.

And he thought, if it was all by chance that he was here, by chance that this great edifice came to be, then nothing mattered. Then it was all the same, whether the toilet gurgled noisily as sewage rose from the ground and he sat at table to expel food onto the plate and wine into the bottle, so that the elevator would carry warm food down to the ground from which faeces had risen.

44

If it was by chance then what did it matter which way the cycle ran, so long as it was a complete cycle? For an incomplete cycle was intolerable even to think about.

If it was by chance then what did it matter if he squeezed through the bars of the window and leapt into the sky?

But if it was by chance then why was it by chance? How was it by chance, this gigantic tower, this marvellous cell, the excellent fare, the incredible table? Why was it by chance, that there were two chairs and one table?

The Tower must exist because of him. How could it be any other way? It could not be that he existed because of the Tower, that perhaps he was to the Tower like the blocks it was made of: Never.

It was not helpful even to think that their existence depended on each other.

If he did not exist, then he would have no way of knowing whether the Tower existed or not. Therefore the Tower could not exist without him: certainly not in the form it did, if he did not exist. It was possible that something might be even without his own existence, but it would only be an amorphous conglomeration of infinite possibilities, which was equivalent to nothing – was perhaps a variant of nothing because nothing could be known about anything in that state.

It was only as a result of his existence and by the astonishing power of observation, that the Tower, the cell and everything in it came to be, selected from the infinite soup of possibilities. Then he was the Creator, the one who called the World from the Dark.

But who called *him* from the Dark?

Yet maybe he was not the cause of it all, but only the reason. How comforting that would be, if he was the reason for it all!

Sometimes he was gripped by a burning passion to discover all: he ran from one side of the cell to the other; he poked his head through the window; he stuck his hand through the door.

Sometimes he did not care at all.

He paced the cell, round and round about in a spiral path; a man in an open orbit. But on the third revolution, as he passed the bars of the door, something at once terrible and sublime happened; something frightful and comforting: something so unprecedented that he stopped in his tracks.

He heard a sound.

For the first time he heard a sound that he had not made, a sound other than the 'ping!' of the elevator or the gurgling of the toilet. He heard a sound other than the rushing wind outside.

Footsteps.

He stood very, very still, holding his breath so that he could hear better. After a while he was certain that it was footsteps, sounding faintly some great distance away.

What did it mean? How did it fit into all this? Was there a plan, after all?

He grasped the bars of the door and listened. He could not tell whether the footsteps came from above or from below. Yet he knew they had to come from below. It made more sense to think that they came from below.

It made sense and it was acceptable and comforting, to think that he was the reason for these footsteps.

A 'ping!' resounded through the cell: Lunch was served. He turned around to see the door of the elevator slide noiselessly open, revealing a loaded tray.

He ate hurriedly, pausing often to listen for the footsteps. He had to eat. If he did not eat then how could he put empty dishes into the elevator? And if he did not put the empty dishes into the elevator then it would not go down. And if the elevator did not go down how could it come up with supper? He had to eat, or he would foul up the process and that would not be good.

His thoughts were all on the footsteps. From below or from above? From below. Who? What?

Those footsteps so far away, heels against the hard stone steps.

Lunch over, he dutifully carried the tray back to the elevator and with a hiss the door slid shut and the spent plates were carried off.

He went to stand beside the door, hugging the cold metal bars till his arms ached. The footsteps did not grow any louder, but neither did they fade off.

He walked across the cell and sat on the one-legged stool. The footsteps were audible from there too, so he decided that the sound was growing louder, though agonisingly slowly.

Many thoughts crowded his mind as he gazed out of the window. What if the sound suddenly ceased? What if the footsteps started receding again? What then would be the meaning of it all?

There was some special significance. Certainly, there was great significance. There were two chairs in his cell and he was the only one in the cell. There was only one set of footsteps. Therefore for the sake of completeness the footsteps had to be destined for his cell. It made sense that way.

He was convinced that many questions would be answered if the footsteps ended at his door.

But among his thoughts there was one that was singularly terrible. What if the footsteps came by his cell and perhaps paused at his door – and then went on?

What if the footsteps came to his door and then went past it?

Would he see who was passing, would he have enough time to run to the door and shout; 'Tell me what this is all about?'

Chapter 7

Twilight

I NO LONGER feel the pain. Something has happened, then, that I am not aware of, that I was not aware of. Perhaps it is an advanced stage.

It is dark in my room, soft in my bed...

Yet why not all these things. I recall some time ago someone said and so we playfully prayed, prayerfully played;

That we might die a quiet death
Peacefully in our beds.

Surely I am in bed. But I cannot tell, perhaps it is just an advanced stage; you got to this stage even if you were pushed out of a speeding train. And run over.

Yet surely I am in bed, quietly lying down, pillow to head, gracefully breathing: no ugliness.

The most terrifying thought is that of slipping into the Loneliness. To be so utterly alone, eternally. To have nothing to relate to; to become nothing except a persistent consciousness and memory; thus for eternity reliving the life gone by and exploring the extent of the

49

mind, but still alone, alone, alone...

Thus one was born to face in the end this dark horror.

I wonder what would be different, as I lie here wondering Dear Martha, if you had when I humbly came to you and said Dear Martha Please Do My Love Accept instead of turning your head up nose up with a supercilious Huh would it have been different now Martha, as my thoughts fall upon you settle upon you Dear Martha even now I cannot deny that Dear Martha My Love Is Ever True.

Nothing would be different, for all will be alone in the end.

And ye shall be as gods, said the serpent. All ate the fruit, but did the serpent eat the fruit of the knowledge, subtle in the Garden? And ye shall be as gods and yet did not eat.

This then must explain the fantastic intelligence of man, the mind and imagination soaring high above even that of the other primates, which, as scientists are at great pains to assure us, are our closest living neighbours on earth, in the solar system, in the Universe.

This be as gods, this knowledge, that one would be and know it too?

Now perhaps the promise of the devil is fulfilled, man becomes like God, existing alone with nothing but the creative power of the imagination. Creation shall take place yet again in my mind. What else would there be to do, faced with grim loneliness for eternity?

That you may be and know it too.

Yet surely I am lying in bed. I no longer feel the pain,

but have only vague memories of some discomfort. It is all gone now.

I have heard about people screaming in sheer fright at the time of death: What could they have seen, that scared them so? The blazing fires of Hell? But Hell after Judgment and not before; someone might have read their Bible wrong.

And those funny smart new Theologians, masters of euphemisms and sweetened pills, who now propose; It might not be fire but a deep eternal sense of loss. What then could those dying have seen, to make them scream? Could it perhaps be simply Goodbye I will miss you Life.

In my past life I must have sinned; yet I feel no guilt and can only remember things I did, not sins I committed. For I also killed a man: the circumstance escapes, unimportant in the face of the fact. My grip on his throat unrelenting, the light faded in his eyes: and he died and I lived.

The accusations of unbelief and the promise of dire consequence come to mind. In past times this was rejected as a needless bother. Yet now...

Yet now
Even as I go
I pray I pray
That He on the Cross
Will hold my hand
And lead me...
...home?

I hear nothing. See nothing. Smell nothing. Feel nothing but the softness of the bed that must be.

Yet my thoughts remain.

Life is a condemned man being led to the gallows. On the way he hears the most sublime music. More than anything he wishes to pause a moment and listen to the music, but the execution cannot be delayed. He is hurried along, while the music plays on.

So perhaps it has happened, how can I tell now? Perhaps even now they close my eyelids and sign the cross over my head. How will I know, how can I know? Perhaps it is over and I am gone...

Only the living can tell who has died.

And with a cry, it must have been, my entry into this one-way road that allows no turning back or standing still: all motion is inexorably forward. And each generation regenerates, does unto others what was done unto them and more souls are saddled with the terrible gift of life.

Finally perhaps, the sum of a man's life is to have done more evil than good unto others, or to have had more evil than good done unto him. Yet neither choice is acceptable. Everyone is equally innocent, yet some pay a huge price for life. Therefore life cannot be a race, because it is not fair.

Do I now list my achievements? Yet what achievement is worthwhile but changes the fundamental misery of humanity: intelligent flotsam but jetsam nonetheless.

Moments of pleasure, of joy – indeed there were several. There were times of excitement, when I rode the adrenalin surge in exhilaration. Under the leafy foliage in the coolness of the night, the word in question is 'fondle': a capacious bosom is recalled, a rapacious attitude remembered.

Then there were the spiritual moments, when in certain transports – as the choir raised a heavenly chorus perhaps – my soul was enraptured and I felt the presence; yea, the very presence.

So now what is there to say – to prattle my biography, tease out choice bits of memory, examine the philosophical pillars of my life? What has it all been about? This is the question that makes me doubt that it has all been worth the time.

I no longer feel the pain. There was a time that I did feel pain, bad pain in my body, in my thoughts. Now the pain no longer, with it the bed no longer, though I insist I am in bed.

In these last moments of the crossover,
This feared, inevitable stage,
This stage now reached, now passed, who can say.

PART II

Paradise By The Dashboard Light

Chapter 8

Mr Happy And The Hammer Of God

I am the eye in the sky, looking at you.
  – *The Alan Parsons Project, 'Eye in the Sky'.*

i. Another Decade of Sunlight

DERVI'S SCREAMS RIPPED through the quiet night as he grabbed the bedpost and pulled himself into a sitting position. Heart pounding, his eyes sought to penetrate the inscrutable darkness. His body was clammy with sweat and the mattress had slid halfway off the bed, a testament to the brutality of the horrors that had flung him out of sleep.

The nightmares had come back with renewed strength.

But the incubus did not need dreams to wreak acts of terror: the night was turf enough. As Dervi gathered the bedclothes around his body to ward off a sudden chill, whispers floated from under the bed and claws scratched at the windowpanes.

Dervi wept, pleading for reprieve.

57

'Leave me alone, leave me alone.'

This did not help: rather the whispers turned into snarls and the scratching into pounding. Dervi did not dare walk across the room to the light switch – because then he would strike and Dervi knew that he would never spare anyone.

Dervi pulled the bed sheets over his head and lay still.

'There is no escape, Dervi.' The whisper carried to him with obscene clarity.

There was a mirthless, sinister chuckling and then the whispers stopped and the pounding died away. Silence reigned in the darkness, but Dervi was still too scared to even shift a limb.

As dawn approached Dervi finally slipped into a deep slumber, from which he was roused by the mid-morning sunlight ravaging his room. It was a great relief to be free from the horrors of darkness. Dervi felt happy even before he became fully aware of the shabby interior of his apartment. He could not remember what the dreams had been about, but he did not care to fill in the blanks.

The dusty black edge of the portable stereo faded into his expanding universe and his fingers sought out the knob. Music blasted forth and cleared the vestiges of sleep from his brain.

The sun struck bright rays through the windowpanes, burning a cheerful yellow into the small apartment, brightening the threadbare couch, exposing breadcrumbs on the wobbly dining table and warming the stale air in the room.

'O the glory of the morning!' Dervi shouted in delight,

stretching until his joints popped. His happiness bubbled from deep within, seeming to have no outward cause.

On the radio, the DJ had caught his mood, laying on track after track of Dervi's favourite music. Springsteen was *Trapped*, ABBA had their *Waterloo*; The Eagles met the *Tequila Sunrise*. Dervi sang along in a loud voice, even though he did not know the words of the songs:

'It's another decade of sunlight and another night of feeling blue, when the sunshine is gone.'

It made little sense, but whether or not he got the words right was not the point; the important thing was that he was singing and he was happy – which was unusual, because he usually felt depressed after a bad dream.

His day began with a mug of strong black coffee, savoured with relish at the dining table. Through the dirt-rimmed window, the poor, congested neighbourhood made a brave showing. In the courtyard of the next house two girls were hanging out washing; barely twenty feet away from them a man urinated carelessly against the wall. Dirty buildings, rusting roofing sheets and a few gallant trees struggling against the man-made barrenness of Abossey-Okai all fought for attention in the little square of glass.

Dervi turned his back to the window. Such sights had the power to spoil his cheerful mood. He did not like being reminded that many people were probably as poor and desperate as he was – maybe even more so – and living in quarters worse than his own mean digs.

Dervi lived on the second – and topmost – floor of an

apartment block whose owners had forgotten the meaning of maintenance. The building was in a bad state, the roof leaked when it rained and the toilets often choked and emitted foul odours.

Apart from the regular visits by his family, no one ever bothered to climb up to his room. Dervi liked it that way. He had only a vague idea of whom his neighbours were; in turn, they did not care to interact with the taciturn, eccentric bachelor in his late twenties who they believed was quite mad.

Today was the last weekday of the month; his monthly appointment with the consultant at the psychiatric hospital was at three-thirty in the afternoon. These meetings were now routine and Dervi looked forward to them, just as a devout Catholic would look forward to High Mass. Yet, he did not like going to the hospital; neither did he like meeting the consultant, although they sometimes had interesting conversations. The consultant was an intelligent person; under different circumstances, he might have been a good friend. But that was now impossible, because the consultant had too much power – he could have Dervi committed, as he had done once before. There cannot be friendship if one party is so much more powerful than the other. Ergo, Dervi thought, Man cannot be friends with God.

Dervi looked forward to the meetings because they were like milestones along the path to recovery. They represented markers to his state of health. Was he getting better? Was he getting worse? Was everything as it was before?

Dervi thought that nothing had changed since the last few meetings. He wondered what the consultant would say this time.

Coffee over, Dervi reached for the small pile of old editions of *Newsweek* and *The Economist*, graciously donated by his father. Whenever the family paid him a visit, they brought along copies of these magazines and some old newspapers as well.

'Certainly one has to keep up-to-date with news and opinions, especially when leaving the domicile to interact with others,' Dervi muttered, settling into the creaky armchair.

The most recent news item was at least two months old, but that was good enough for Dervi. He could have requested current copies of the news journals, but then the gloomy current affairs of the world would depress him. Old news could do no harm.

He had read some articles several times over, but he did not mind reading them again. A particularly hilarious entertainment review in *Newsweek* was a must-read before leaving for the hospital.

This was what he began with, chortling his way through the article, remembering how he had chortled through the same article, seated in the same armchair, over and over again every month for five months in succession.

Dervi had lunch at two o'clock – a miserly affair of yesterday's leftovers – followed by a quick bath in the smelly bathroom. Then he proceeded to dress up, selecting a white cotton shirt and a pair of black trousers from the wardrobe.

'Migod!' Dervi swore, examining the shirt. 'This garment has developed a fault!' He picked at the frayed cuffs. 'But it does not matter too much. The trousers are in great shape and the shoes are new. It balances.'

He wanted everything to be perfect, so that no one would have cause to point a finger at him. Certainly, it was also necessary to try out his gait. Dervi took practice steps around the room.

'Bold!' he barked, marching into the kitchen with chest thrust forward, swinging stiff arms. The black shoes shone with a gloss worthy of a military recruit.

'Suave,' he crooned, swaggering his return to the bedroom, one hand thrust into a trouser pocket, right eyebrow cocked. He stopped in front of the mirror and put on a pair of dark sunglasses. A partially reformed gangster looked back from the mirror, obviously proud of his Afro-styled hair: the four-inch high bush exuded an impressive sheen, a testament to careful grooming.

Everything was satisfactory, Dervi thought, slinging a worn satchel over his shoulder and stepping out of the room. He went down a short, dismal corridor and into the gloomy stairwell. The electric wires there had burnt out long ago.

He met no one during his descent into the walled courtyard, itself in shadow due to the huge mango tree leaning across the small space. He crossed quickly, keeping his eyes directly on the rusted iron gates; this was an exit to freedom.

Going through the gates was like stepping into a TV screen; Dervi entered a different world altogether. The street was busy, people hurried by, cars crawled along, the sound of traffic filled the air. But best of all, the sun blazed away in mid-sky. Dervi loved the flaming orb when it appeared in fiery glory like today. Whenever old Sol was burning bright and making him squint, Dervi was sure that there was no God; and because there was no God, there was no Devil, no heaven nor hell nor life after death. His mind could be at peace.

The entire trip to the hospital would take twenty minutes by bus, or thirty minutes, giving allowance for traffic hold-ups somewhere along the road. His route was well planned. He first had to walk to Obetsebi Lamptey Circle, get onto a bus and head north-east along the Ring Road to Kwame Nkrumah Circle, from where a taxi would bear him directly to the Accra Psychiatric Hospital.

The traffic situation at Obetsebi Lamptey Circle was close to pandemonium. Cars were locked bumper-to-bumper and drivers shouted themselves hoarse in vain. A man in a suit – looking every bit the business executive – had left his air-conditioned BMW and was having an altercation with a taxi driver. There obviously had been a case of bad driving.

'You drive like...like an imbecile!' the business executive huffed, wagging a finger at the driver, who replied by leaning out and yelling for everyone to hear:

'Imbecile...Your mother...!'

The man's eyebrows shot up as he choked at this challenge. Dervi half expected a lunge for the throat of his vituperative opponent, but at that moment the cars began crawling forward. A myriad of car horns blasted impatiently as the business executive made a desperate dash for his BMW. The taxi drew away, leaving him fumbling at the steering wheel.

Dervi chuckled his way past the scene. His bus stop was away from all the noise and confusion. Ten minutes later, he was at the Kwame Nkrumah Circle bus terminus.

An ancient blue-and-yellow taxi was waiting for one more passenger. The battered vehicle looked like a Fiat but might actually have been something else during its long life, since every part of it must have been replaced at least once. Dervi slipped into the front seat, pleased not to have to join a queue, as was often the case. Three stern-faced young men who looked like secret service agents occupied the back seat; looking resolute in white shirts, navy-blue ties and sunglasses.

The driver was a gnarled old man. His hair was streaked with white and a surprisingly luxuriant beard gave him a sage-like aura, though the effect was spoilt because instead of a serene look of wisdom, his face was creased in a perpetually anxious expression. This was probably because the ancient jalopy seemed to have a life of it's own, which life often veered towards expiration. As the car sputtered along, the man complained about traffic hold-ups and cursed at every red light.

'Look ooh,' he said, when the car ahead did not go as quickly as he would have wished. 'Look at that foolish one too.'

The taxi jerked and almost stalled as it pulled away

from a traffic intersection. Dervi wondered how fast the car could really go. Obviously, the old man's faith in his car seemed misplaced. Maybe not, Dervi thought: only heaven knows what the two of them have been through together.

ii. The Consultation

The taxi rattled to a stop, its engine wheezing and coughing. Dervi looked at himself in the rear-view mirror before stepping out, ignoring the angry 'Quick, hurry up and go' glance of the driver. He always felt self-conscious outside the psychiatric hospital, having never got over the fear that someone he knew might see him and conclude that he was nuts. An absurd thought, since most of his acquaintances knew that he had had a mental breakdown. Nevertheless, he still felt vulnerable to prying eyes as he quickly crossed the road.

'THE PSYCHIATRIC HOSPITAL, ACCRA', declared a large signboard at the entrance. Dervi barely noticed that the walls had acquired a new coat of paint as he hastened through the shabby metal gates.

Just ahead of him, a surly faced orderly prodded a young man along. Probably the man had run wild, because he was restrained with loops of nylon rope tied around him. His muscular arms twitched under the knots, which bit cruelly into the glistening skin. Dervi drew up to the pair and the man turned towards him, his eyes screaming for help. What has he done? Dervi thought, reaching out to touch the rope, but the orderly glared at him, eyes widening threateningly. Dervi quickened his pace. Behind him, there was a whimper of despair and a brutally uttered 'Move!'

Dervi felt sad. I wish I could cut you free, he thought. But I am also bound; only you cannot see the ropes.

He headed straight for the consulting rooms, his shoes passing swiftly over the worn concrete floor of a long corridor. Cobwebs clung desperately to the edges of the ceiling. To his left there was a patch of dusty ground, better put to growing a lawn. The consulting rooms were to his right, door after door along the corridor. Dervi's consultant was behind one of these ignominious yellow doors shyly recessed in the tired green wall, which was streaked with dirt and had many discoloured patches. The white nameplate on the door bore imposing black letters declaring:

Polduous, PhD. Consulting Psychiatrist.

Dervi called the consultant Pol – it was so much simpler.

There were five people seated on the long wooden bench in front of the consulting room. The man sitting closest to the door stared vacuously at the paint peeling off the ceiling, next to him a geriatric laboured over a newspaper, mumbling, stumbling over the words. A young lady sitting beside the old man slobbered into a large blue handkerchief while a woman, looking distraught behind age-worn spectacles, occasionally patted her on the back. The geriatric tried to block this sight by turning the sheets in her direction, but this worked slightly to his disadvantage as well, because he had to twist his neck to read the page. At the end of the queue a fat man in a dirty T-shirt gnawed pensively at his lip while patting the bench, making a flat pat-pat-pat sound.

Dervi greeted them with a confident 'Hello!', waving his hospital card in their faces. They muttered crazy responses as he took his place beside the nervous youth at the end of the queue.

A woman emerged from the consulting room, smiling broadly as if all her problems were over. She giggled girlishly when Dervi caught her eye.

The man at the head of the queue was so engrossed in staring at the ceiling that he had to be prodded to mind his turn. Finally aware of what was happening, he rose, offered an apology and marched into the consulting room.

Soon it came to Dervi's turn and then he was the one pushing the yellow door open. It was three forty-five; the meeting was only fifteen minutes overdue. That was all right by Dervi. He recalled a time when he had been kept waiting for more than an hour because the consultant had had 'unexpected difficulties' with a client.

Much effort had been put into making the room cheerful and welcoming. The curtains were brightly coloured and there were picturesque landscapes on the white walls. The consultant looked up from behind a large, cluttered up desk and said, 'Good afternoon. Please be seated.'

Dervi sat down on a straight-backed chair opposite

Pol. A pleasant gust of cool air coursed down from the air conditioner fixed high on the wall.

Pol's thick eyebrows puckered over the rim of his spectacles. His hair was close cropped and his face bore no trace of a moustache or beard. This made his unusually bushy eyebrows stand out. Pol had a habit of wiggling his eyebrows as he spoke. The agility of the little tufts of hair was rather astonishing; watching them often distracted Dervi from the conversation.

Pol turned his attention to a file on his desk. He made a note in it before pushing it aside and reaching for another. Pol frowned and Dervi began to fear that the consultant might be in a bad mood. Dervi clasped his hands and looked at the carefully arranged volumes in the bookcase. A fresh cutting of red and yellow bougainvillea poked out of a blue ceramic vase on the topmost shelf.

Finally Pol raised his head.

'Pardon me,' he said. 'I just had to complete that.' The voice was gentle and pleasant. 'How are you today?'

'Everything is still the same,' Dervi replied, feeling a little uneasy.

'That is good. You know, things could have become worse.'

Dervi said nothing. It was always like this when he met Pol; one had to be careful. At the beginning of the interaction, he had to gauge the mood of the consultant and structure his responses properly, because Pol had the power to consign him to the madhouse – and Dervi knew that was a terrible place to be. He kept quiet, allowing Pol to speak. If it turned out that the consultant was amenable to conversation, they would talk as one man to another and not man to madman. Man to madman occurred at the beginning of the interaction, man to man at the end.

Pol asked some questions about his health. Dervi replied a little cautiously: it was necessary to remember the important details; besides, he had to choose his words carefully in order not to give Pol the wrong impression. There had been no particularly worrisome illness during the period – headaches were not to be considered, of course, there was aspirin for that – so he did not mention that he sometimes went to bed with a bad headache. His dreams had mostly been evil, as usual. They were nightmares, replete with demons, Hellfire and heavily punctuated with the presence of a judgmental, merciless God who seemed incapable of understanding Dervi. Long ago Dervi had told Pol about his dreams.

'They usually end with some sort of a judgement scene – a figure I cannot properly describe appears and I hear a shout: "Guilty as charged!" and another voice says, "Now Dervi, depart you to Hell, prepared for the devil and his angels." Then I try to explain myself, beg for a fair hearing. I cry, "It's not fair!" In any case, since I am neither the devil nor one of his angels, why must I go there? But no matter what I say, despite all my protests, I feel a blast of red heat and know that I have been cast down.'

Pol's response had been a little disappointing. Dervi had expected more than the cursory sympathy the man showed; he had expected a full discussion of the metaphorical significance of the dreams: he wanted an interpretation. 'Very interesting,' Pol had replied. 'But I am afraid this sort of thing is not exactly my speciality – I am more of a "chemicals" person – you know, prescription drugs, not psychoanalysis. Perhaps if I recommend a meeting with . . . '

'That's quite all right,' Dervi quickly interjected. 'I am sure that the medication will resolve the problem entirely.'

'Well, if it doesn't – and of course we'll monitor the dreams – if it doesn't, you should consider seeing our specialist.'

Since then, Dervi had not bothered Pol with details of the dreams again. He was on medication now. The dreams had not gone away.

Sometimes they were ordinary, gentle dreams; sometimes they were violent dreams of the sort he had described. Lately, Dervi had begun to suspect that the medication might actually be part of the problem – he decided to mention it to Pol today.

The consultant was jotting down some points as he listened to Dervi's replies.

'Thank you.' Pol said. 'Now, what are your plans as to becoming employed again?'

The question surprised Dervi. Does the man not understand that I am unwell? he thought. The thought became a voice, sounding so loud in his head – 'Can you not see that I am ill?' – Dervi was not sure whether he had spoken or not. But he probably hadn't, because Pol still prodded:

'Have you considered it?'

Dervi replied, rather flippantly:

'Really, I do not care.' He had now gained enough confidence to look Pol straight in the eye.

'That is not good,' Pol returned. 'Please, keep thinking about this. It is very important for your re-integration into society.'

'Who wants to be re-integrated into society?' Dervi challenged. 'Society is just a dressed up ulcer.'

Pol hmm-hmm-ed.

'Now why is that?' he asked cautiously.

'Everybody is sick! Can you not see that?'

'Everybody is not "sick", Dervi. A few people have conditions that prevent them from integrating properly into society. Fortunately, science has found ways of helping such individuals, many of whom have completely recovered.'

'And many of whom walk the dark dungeons of institutions.'

Pol smiled thinly. 'Your language is rather colourful,' he said. 'But these are not dungeons.'

'But the science fails, nevertheless.'

'Sadly, though we try our best, the cases are sometimes beyond our capacity to resolve.'

Dervi was feeling irritated at Pol's cool PR manner. He felt like baring his buttocks and farting at the consultant, just to make him speak from the heart. Now, the man sounded like a textbook. An angry voice whispered in Dervi's mind, 'The man is so blasé. Does he not realise that this is my life?'

Dervi leaned forward, speaking with an air of grave

finality as if revealing a profound secret:

'The system is sick... rotten throughout. The fact that people end up malfunctioning should tell you this. Society screws people up... forces them to be some sort of special animal. Those who fail to conform end up here, like me. But it is not my fault. Never, never! From the start, I have been innocent. I reject any blame.'

Pol replied, 'Innocent from the start, maybe. But at some point you assumed responsibility for your actions. By making your choices, you became the one to carry the blame. This is a fact. Accept it; it will help in your recovery.'

Dervi was not moved by this argument.

'Yes, but what about predestination? I am convinced that our lives are predestined; some souls are doomed to the dungeons, to Hell – right from the start. They cannot be blamed.'

'I am not qualified to discuss theology.' Pol returned, in the same cool manner.

Pol tilted his capacious chair backwards. Dervi glowered at the consultant for a short while; then he also leaned back. His chair creaked. The consultant had one of those large, padded, executive swivel chairs that were much touted for their ergonomics. Dervi's chair was a much more humble straight-backed affair; the cushion was even lumpy in some places. He shifted uncomfortably, enviously watching Pol swing his chair gently from side to side. The consultant's forehead creased in contemplation and his eyebrows met over his nose.

Finally, Pol said, 'I can see that religious matters are

very important to you. I suggest that you consider passing by a church – have a meeting with the pastor, maybe. There is a Christian Mission working with some of the inmates here. If you wish, I ...'

'...could make a recommendation.' Dervi finished for Pol.

'Definitely,' Pol said.

The consultant was so predictable. If it were not his area of specialisation, he would give a recommendation. If it was his field, he would give advice and of course, medication.

'I still stand by my initial proposition,' Dervi insisted. 'And I challenge you to prove that it is I, rather than society, that is ill.'

'And such a proof, how will it help you?' Pol asked.

'If I am not the one that is ill, but instead society is ill, then my medication is misdirected.'

Pol replied with a one-sided smile that stretched his left cheek. His eyebrows straightened out.

'It is possible that society is also ill. Yet, there are no pills available for society.'

'But there are pills for me.' Dervi said.

'Precisely.'

'Damnation,' Dervi swore. 'The whole enterprise is worthless.'

'Don't give up,' Pol said. 'It is not helpful to make yourself unhappy. Though it is impossible for a person to be happy all the time; one must nevertheless pursue happiness.'

'I have pursued happiness before.' Dervi replied.

'Those activities were similar to a response to fear: you were running away from something. Not looking for happiness.'

'All those women,' Dervi murmured.

'Exactly.'

An image of a woman's naked bottom faded into Dervi's mind. He shook his head to get rid of it. The consultant had it all wrong. Dervi knew that he had been trying to make himself happy. But he could never fully describe the dark despair he used to feel while alone, when terrible chasms opened up in his mind and he had to be happy or die. His girlfriends had provided a channel for resolution, although these periods of sadness were more frequent and intense when he was with them. Sex had not presented a total solution, but it worked as an immediate and effective palliative.

'I still think it was a pursuit of happiness.' Dervi insisted.

Pol replied, 'To seek instant gratification without thinking about the future is a typical reaction to consistent high stress.'

Dervi shut his eyes and asked dreamily, his voice dropping to a murmur:

'What is happiness? Is happiness the sole objective in life? Everyone does what they do, simply to be happy...! People want to go to heaven, because they want to be happy, forever... not because they want to see God, but only because they will be happy when they do... Is life all about happiness? Huh? Is it? Is it?'

'I think that happiness is an important objective in life.

One cannot live to be unhappy. That is also a mental condition, an illness.' Pol replied.

'Yes, but is happiness all there is? Is it the highest?' Dervi asked, thinking how trite life would be, if happiness were the pinnacle. Then all that was needed would be the Happy Pill and the lights could be turned off. Nobody would complain. Yet, a person had to be free from pain. That much, at least, was necessary.

'I'm afraid I'm not qualified to discuss philosophy.' Pol's sensible voice reached into Dervi's thoughts and plucked him firmly back into the consulting room. A waft of cool air passed over his face again. The two men considered each other thoughtfully.

Dervi said, 'If one cannot be happy all the time then I must stop taking the medication; it is useless. In any case, it makes me sleepless and then when I manage to sleep I have terrible nightmares about God. I have also lost appetite for food and I think that the medication has made the nightmares worse.'

'I doubt that the medication has made the nightmares worse,' Pol began. 'We'll have to monitor that over the next month. The general side effects of the medication are easily dealt with, as we have discussed before. You must understand that the medication is not to make you ... laugh all the time. It is meant to correct a chemical dysfunction so that you can face the challenges of life. I insist that you should continue taking the medication. It has helped you; I can see that. Then again, you will get worse if you quit and if you get much worse, we will have you committed.'

'What a terrible thing to say,' Dervi said.

Pol did not reply. He looked diminutive on the other side of the cluttered desk. Dervi knew that the interview was over. He wondered if he had made a good impression on the consultant.

Pol was speaking again.

'In the final analysis, your condition has improved. Definitely, we did the right thing by putting you on medication. It also encourages me to increase the dosage slightly. Please note the new dose – the pharmacist will show you.'

He began filling a prescription form.

'What a terrible thing to say,' Dervi repeated.

Pol stopped writing and twirled the pen. His eyebrows pulled together: he seemed to be making a decision.

'Yes, isn't it,' he finally said.

'You lied.' Dervi told him. 'I am not getting any better.'

Pol continued filling out the form.

iii. Farewell Till We Meet Again

Dervi thought that the meeting had gone rather well – if for nothing at all Pol had let him go and not confined him within these walls, where life would have been bitter indeed. Clutching the prescription form, Dervi left the office and as the door clicked gently shut behind him, his gaze swept over the people waiting outside. The queue had grown again; four other people were sitting on the bench. He turned away with a sprightly step, feeling triumphant – he had seen the consultant before they had.

At the dispensing pharmacy, there was yet another small group of people waiting, but the atmosphere was more relaxed than it had been in front of Pol's office. It was easy to understand why. Here people had come to pick up, in a medicine bottle, the resolution to their problems. Their ills had been diagnosed and they had hope of a cure, or at least a palliative for their condition. Once they got to this place, the situation was not out-of-hand; there was hope.

Dervi wrinkled his nose at the odour – an indeterminate smell of disinfectant and strangely enough, of expectorant. It was the kind of smell characteristic of a place like this. He pushed the prescription through the little window in the screen behind the counter. This screen, made of ceiling-high slats of plywood, was painted a meaningless shade of green and blocked the view across the counter. He sat down and waited for the medication to be served. After about five minutes, someone called his name. Dervi went back to the little window. A woman's hand pushed the medication onto the counter. The pharmacist was hidden from the client; their interaction was limited to voices and to the sight of one hand. It was a clever little scheme for maintaining some privacy. Dervi thought it was a rather agreeable one at that. For all he could tell, it was his former classmate behind the screen and he had no wish to speak to his former classmate.

The medicine bottle fitted into his satchel so Dervi did not need the proffered plastic bag, which he pushed back with a rather boisterous 'Thank you.'

No one replied; the pharmacist had gone away. Dervi left

the dispensary. It was over for today, for this month: now he had to go back home. The sunlight was not as bright as before, but it made him squint any way. He reached into his pocket and was alarmed not to find the sunglasses. His brow creased in thought. Where could they be?

Dervi returned to the dispensary and looked about the place where he had been sitting, scanning the counter as well. The sunglasses were not there. People looked at him curiously, but no one asked him anything. He was pleased not to have to speak, for was it not obvious that he was looking for something?

The only other place he could have left the sunglasses was Pol's office. Dervi was relieved when he remembered this. That had to be the place; he had been wearing the glasses when he entered and naturally would have put them on Pol's desk. Of course, that was it. He smiled at himself as he made his way back to the consulting room.

The four people sitting on the bench wore forlorn expressions – he saw despair, impatience and even suicide – written on their faces. Dervi felt bad about crossing the queue. It was not their fault that he had forgotten the sunglasses, he thought. In any case, he had had his turn; it was only fair that they had theirs undisturbed. Dervi halted just in front of the door, turned around and nodding at the people in the queue, made his way back. However, once in the sun again, he reconsidered his action. Returning to Pol's office was not going to cause any major disruption, was it? He would spend less than a minute. He would only say,

'Beg your pardon, Pol, I left my glasses on your desk.'

And Pol would reply kindly, handing the piece over: 'Yes, you did. Here they are.' Then Dervi would leave. It was a very simple matter. No one would be hurt or need be angry.

Once again Dervi turned and stepped briskly towards the consulting room and once again he faltered at the sight of the unhappy people sitting there. To interrupt the process would only bring grief, he thought. Some of those people were so much more ill than he was. 'Be fair! Be magnanimous', a voice in his head encouraged him. After all, it was just a cheap pair of sunglasses, costing about two cedis. Besides, Pol would probably keep them for him until their next meeting in four weeks' time.

Sighing, Dervi made an about face once more. He pushed thoughts of the sunglasses out of his mind by trying to remember the words of Tequila Sunrise, played on the radio that morning. He passed through the shabby metal gates and set off for the bus stop, which was only a short walk away.

A woman in tattered clothes detached herself from the crowd of street peddlers and beggars and came up to him. She exuded an unpleasant odour. Her hair was unkempt; she obviously had not washed for some time. Yet she was young; could not be more than twenty-five. Dervi wondered; why was she like this? Her life stood like the open highway, years and years of living before her. How could she continue like this?

'Dear sir,' said the woman in a voice that warbled. Her breath stank of something rotten.

Dervi wanted to cry.

'Hello,' he said. There was no sun in his voice.

'Money,' she said simply.

Dervi reached into his pocket and found only a single bill in it: Five cedis, intended for the trip home and for supper. The woman snatched it greedily from his hand and scampered off without even a 'thank you'. But Dervi was not offended, although he had lost his supper and now had to walk home. There was nothing for it, he thought. Things like this happened all the time. It was not all bad; people could go through hell and still come out with their humanity intact.

Dervi would really have loved to wear his sunglasses now that he had to walk all the way to Abossey-Okai, but he rejected the thought of going back to Pol's office.

He headed west along Castle Road, treading homeward with a bold and steady step.

There was a traffic intersection at the Cathedral Square less than twenty metres ahead and a little further across the road, to the right, stood the Cathedral itself.

iv. The Cathedral

Crossing the Square, Dervi could not ignore the ecclesiastical edifice looming to his right, pitifully grey in the cheerful light. A few windows of coloured glass turned like blind eyes onto the street; the wall bore a huge white concrete dove descending, underneath which some ugly brown doors declared an entrance. A squat tower thrust a lonely cross into the air. Dervi felt an urge to turn right, deviate from his path and go through the gates into the cathedral courtyard.

There was a man in a cassock wandering about in the dusty car park. The Cathedral, seen from close quarters, looked sad and tired. Dervi marched up to the lone priest and said sternly:

'You dog, eunuch for the sake of God, sit there on that stone and let us talk.'

The priest seemed rather surprised. His thin lips drew into a gentle smile and he asked in a friendly manner:

'How may I help you?'

The priest was taller than Dervi. His neck was long and thin, with a protuberant Adam's apple that wobbled when he spoke.

'Be seated!' Dervi repeated, pointing at a rock the size of a basketball poking out of the ground. The priest was initially hesitant, but Dervi's fierce mien and commanding posture – finger pointed directly at the rock, jaw tilted menacingly – made the priest comply. Dervi waited impatiently for the man to sit down before he began speaking.

'It is easy to understand that in the land of the blind, a one-eyed man is most likely to be misunderstood, derided, declared insane and condemned to death. Today's question is whether Jesus Christ was a one-eyed man.'

Seeing the priest flinch, Dervi paused for a moment before going on:

'Yes. He was a one-eyed man, perhaps the ultimate one-eyed man and he suffered the fate of such. Yet, the followers of a one-eyed man are not necessarily one-eyed;

81

this is the problem with you. Some followers may be one-eyed themselves, but the vast majority can only have faith in the original vision of the one-eyed man, or they can pretend. But with faith must come humility and this is the true test for the follower of the one-eyed man who in the case of Christ cannot be one-eyed himself. Humility! Are you humble?'

Dervi took a deep breath; the speech had him rather winded. The priest looked frightened. He clasped his hands in a prayerful gesture.

'Answer me!' Dervi insisted, pleased with the impact of his words.

'I am afraid for you,' the priest said.

'Of, or for?'

'For.'

'Why?'

'You are from the place across the road, where they try to cure the ills of your mind. Here, Christ offers a cure for the ills of your soul. You calmly listen to the ministrations of the psychiatrist, but then you burst in here, to challenge God. How can you be healed?'

'Today's topic is, "The One-eyed Man". You digress. This is a red herring! We are not talking about healing.'

'If you are not healed, how can you argue?'

'You are not co-operating,' Dervi began angrily, then suddenly cried, 'Take that!' and kicked the priest just below the left ear.

The priest screamed as he went sprawling into the dirt.

'Yes,' Dervi said. 'You listen to me now.'

The priest rose slowly to his feet, the white cassock

smudged with dirt.

'Why have you assaulted me?' he asked hoarsely, holding his head. 'It is dislocated,' he complained.

'It is still there,' Dervi said.

'You are a violent man.' The priest declared.

'Get thee back on the stone!' Dervi commanded, feeling the thrill of power surging up his spine, making him invincible. The priest sat down, looking frightened and miserable.

'This is the payback!' Dervi declared, facing the priest squarely and bringing his palm and fist together with a loud slap. 'Yes! For your lies, hurting me through all the years. First you make me ill and then you offer to heal. You want me to walk from this building to the one across the road and then back again. Back and forth from the shrink to you, the mind and the soul; back and forth across the road, the madhouse to the church.'

'I have done nothing.' The priest said.

Dervi would have none of it.

'I can kick with my left foot,' he warned. 'You still have the other cheek.'

The other bowed his head meekly and began shaking the dirt from the cassock.

Dervi asked, 'Do you not think that your God ought to be ashamed of himself? Or at least, remorseful, since His scheme is not working; the world despairs of happiness.'

'What do you mean, my God?'

'There are many Gods.'

'Well, then: my God has nothing to be ashamed of, or

sorry for. He is the supreme God, the Creator; He does not owe anyone anything at all. On the contrary.'

'A creature cannot owe its creator.' Dervi challenged.

'Its existence is at least a debt.'

'It's a two-way debt, or it is no debt at all.'

'It is one way, my friend! And to you, which is the true God?' The man looked up at Dervi, with head cocked. He squinted slightly in the sun; this accentuated his frown.

Dervi cleared his throat. He considered the question as rather important and worthy of a learned, if possible flamboyant, answer. He replied, fixing the priest with a stare which he hoped carried an overwhelming authority: 'A Deity is the expression of the social conscience, so every society has its own true Gods, which inevitably bear the characteristics of its peculiar evolutionary traits. Though God always seems to have human attributes, this is merely due to humanity's narrow imagination. God could just as well have been a star, a supercomputer, or a gene. But you have condemned as devilry any of the gods I could have identified with, forcing me to internalise your foreign God. Sadly, internalising your concept of God is like swallowing a hand-grenade.'

'How can a man swallow a grenade?' the priest challenged.

'Figuratively, figuratively,' Dervi said. 'I know that normally, a grenade cannot be swallowed.'

'Then your metaphor fails.' The man returned. 'It must be disallowed.'

Dervi gave a sarcastic laugh before continuing. 'But tell

me, do you agree that Christ died to redeem mankind?'

'Absolutely.' The priest replied.

'Because of the love of the Godhead.'

'Yes.'

'Why then can a man not seek the face of God directly? Why, for a God that so loves the world, must a man seek assistance from His mother, people that have died and politicians in funny hats, just to have audience?'

'No one has said that man cannot seek God directly.'

'And all these mediators?'

'Be careful not to deride things that are older than you, that have persisted through the ages. Do not rubbish things that your small mind cannot comprehend. Be patient, be humble.' There was a plaintive note in the priest's voice.

'I was the one who told you about humility!' Dervi pointed out robustly.

'Now tell me why, after Christ has died and sins been pardoned, must one still seek forgiveness from a man – a mere mortal, who in any case must also confess to another man. Does the Top Hat also seek forgiveness from yet another?'

'Who is the Top Hat?'

'The Vicar.'

'No man has the power to forgive sins.'

Dervi laughed.

'Except by delegation,' he said.

The other watched him grimly.

'Your sins drive you away from God,' he said. 'You can see this, except that you have set yourself on the path to

Hell, rejecting even the good sense of mediation. I beg you, leave off these blasphemous thoughts and seek God truthfully. These are the Last Days; the return of Christ is imminent. If anything, your hard heart is good evidence.'

'I doubt that you yourself believe in the last days.'

'I have christened babies, married couples and buried the dead – ' the other began.

'All in your short life,' Dervi interjected dryly.

' – And I can tell you, Life is not a joke, as you seem to find it.'

'On the contrary, it is the biggest joke of all.' Dervi said. 'And now I must leave.'

The priest became very agitated. His Adam's apple bobbed up and down as he struggled to find the right words, looking up at Dervi with a forlorn expression, eyes filled with pity. He wrung his hands desperately. Finally, he cried:

'May God have mercy upon you! May the Holy Mother pray for you!'

This irritated Dervi; out of spite, he kicked the priest's head again, this time with his left foot. The priest fell off the stone, whimpering 'Lord have mercy' over and over again. Dervi thought that the first kick had been nicer, because then the priest had screamed in pain.

Standing on the pavement in front of the cathedral, Dervi laughed so much that he gasped for breath, with one hand on his stomach. He had imagined the entire episode and had not moved at all. Though he did not realise it, he had been staring at the building for several minutes. Passers-by leered knowingly, but no one spoke to him.

Dervi strode off. According to his philosophy, when the sun was shining brightly God did not exist. So there was no problem; it was all a game. The event was behind him; the future lay ahead. The pills in his satchel guaranteed happiness; his mind could turn and turn the foundations of the universe and he would bask in the starlight of the glory of man until he was content. He would be occupied until he died.

The grey, grey walls of the Cathedral no longer made much impact on him. Perhaps, it was because the building was not imposing from this side of the road; perhaps it was because of his irreverence.

As usual, the neem trees along Castle Road were flourishing, the leaves cutting out the glare of sunlight and providing a pleasant shade. Cars drove by and destitute people roamed about aimlessly. A man had fallen asleep under one of the trees, with a multicoloured cloth bag propped against the trunk serving as a pillow. Beggars and hawkers clustered around cars held up by the traffic lights.

Dervi spotted some young girls in school uniform coming towards him. He could not help looking at them; looking so fresh, young and pretty, they seemed very happy. They were chattering animatedly, but when they noticed his gaze, they became quiet.

'Good afternoon, young ladies,' he said respectfully, as the girls passed by. One of them must have responded, because Dervi heard a shyly uttered 'Good afternoon.'

But then they giggled and then they laughed, friskily

running a little as if to increase the distance between themselves and Dervi. He did not turn around; he knew that they were laughing at him. He glanced cursorily at his attire. Was he not well dressed? Or had he forgotten to comb his hair again? That could not be so; he had groomed himself before leaving home. Maybe it was something in his face; perhaps he looked gaunt because he had not been eating well and had lost weight.

Yet, was that reason enough to be mocked in the streets? Maybe he should not have spoken to them. But he only did so because they looked so pretty and so happy; by interacting with them, he hoped to share in their light.

A nearby school must have closed for the day, because another group of schoolgirls was approaching him. This time Dervi looked down at the ground and did not raise his eyes until they had passed.

He remembered when he had been in Secondary School – which he had entered as a brilliant, polite and amiable little fellow, but had come out different: still brilliant, polite and amiable – better educated, certainly, but with darkness in his soul. At that time he had been a devout Catholic, but in the following years at the University, he found himself slowly drifting away from the faith. Dervi had left Secondary School with a great dread of demonic attack. Initially he sought protection by steeping himself in religion, but his best friend Bubu encouraged him to overcome his fear by ditching religion altogether. Herself an atheist, Bubu often argued with Dervi about religion, which she thought Dervi would do better without. They discussed his fear of demons during one of their late night strolls about the University campus. The conversation had gone back and forth and around in circles; it had grown warm and cold and they still hadn't agreed on anything. Finally, Bubu turned to him and placed her hand gently on his chest, narrowing her eyes.

'You are driven about in fear because you believe in these phantoms. If you take the bold step into rationality and cast off these weird beliefs, you will be free. Things that do not exist cannot threaten you.' Bubu said.

The full moon lit up the landscape with a silvery light that glimmered in Bubu's eyes. She was wearing a long black dress that clung to her body, outlining her frugal hips and small breasts. Her face was raised and he could see the outline of the nostrils above her full lips. The sexuality of the scene was buried beneath the subject of discussion and the otherworldly ambience of moonlight and silence made Bubu look utterly trustworthy, like a fairy about to lead an imprisoned soul to freedom.

Dervi mumbled something about the benefits of being a Christian. Bubu replied,

'It's all a question of perspective, telling yourself things to make you comfortable. If, as a devout Christian, you face "trials" and "tribulations" – in other words, when the world screws you – you are encouraged to "bear your cross", for of course the Lord knows best. If you are an "unbeliever" facing tough times, it is pointed out to you that your sins cannot be helping you; certainly, you carry a heavy burden because you have rejected Christ. If you are a Christian and you prosper, certainly the grace of the

Lord is upon you. If you prosper and are an unbeliever, you are encouraged to learn from Dives, the rich man who ignored beggars at his table, ending up tormented in Hades. Finally, of course, you will go to Hell if you die unsaved. Which is terrible, definitely – condemned to fire and brimstone forever. Grim.'

Dervi could not recall how that particular discussion had ended. It was likely that they had decided to let the matter rest and had gone on to savour the magic of the beautiful night.

On another occasion, she thought it was necessary to explain that she was not engaged in an open challenge of church doctrine; she pointed out that she was not actively propagating her thoughts.

'A heresiarch? Myself? No, no. I merely want to exercise my personal freedom to question, to think, to understand. Surely, God will not be displeased because I challenge someone's religious ideas? Besides, we cannot know God. We can only pretend.'

Dervi was often swayed by her arguments. The challenge he offered to Bubu was along these lines:

'Christ offers peace to those who follow him. He provides direction in a confusing world. He protects us. He guarantees us eternal life in heaven.'

They argued many times over these things.

One day Dervi asked a question that stalled Bubu.

'Are you happy with yourself?'

This was when the concept of happiness was gradually becoming more important to Dervi. He thought that happiness was one of the ultimate goals of life and he

90

sought to understand the question, 'What is Happiness?'

She paused. 'How do you mean?'

'Are you happy with your life?'

She turned away, cracked her knuckles.

'I don't know,' she returned finally. 'I don't think so. But it is not important, is it?'

'I don't know either,' Dervi replied.

'But why do you ask?'

'Life must have some meaning.' Dervi began, unsure of what he wanted to say.

'That is why people seek God,' Bubu said.

'You have just spent time deriding the importance of religion . . . '

'I did not say religion was not important. I only pointed out some difficulties with religious doctrine. One should seek God without getting a headache as a result.'

In time, Bubu won him over. Dervi shifted his beliefs around to match Bubus'; they became an unbelieving pair, asking many questions and getting no answers.

v. The Banker

Dervi made steady progress, soon reaching the intersection between Castle Road and Kwame Nkrumah Avenue. The sedate motor traffic now took on a characteristic big-city urgency – horns tooted, a multitude of engines roared and the unpleasant tang of exhaust fumes stung the nostrils.

Dervi's route lay south along this road; he would walk to the intersection with Graphic Road and then turn right and head north-west to Obetsebi Lamptey Circle.

There are many banks along Kwame Nkrumah Avenue. Ghana Commercial Bank. Barclays Bank. Merchant Bank. National Investment Bank. Trust Bank. Standard Chartered Bank. All the way from Kwame Nkrumah Circle to Rawlings' Park, bank after bank after bank. Walking on, Dervi remembered gloomily how not too long ago, he used to sit in an air-conditioned room within an office block just like one of these polished glass-and-tile buildings, drinking coffee and tapping away at a computer keyboard. He was then working in a bank, slaving long hours and making quite a bit of money.

After graduating from University, Dervi floundered about for more than one year in search for a job. His applications were rejected so many times that he slowly lost faith in his Bachelor's degree. However, his fortunes turned when he concluded that the orthodox means of seeking a job would not help. He leant rather heavily on a well-placed but distant aunt; she grudgingly used her 'connections' to his benefit. Dervi was amazed at how easy it was. Apparently, it only took a few telephone calls. Within one month he joined the bank as a Customer Service officer.

Anxious to make a good impression, Dervi attacked the job with such dedication that after a year he was moved to one of the high profile branches on High Street. Whispers suggesting an imminent promotion hung in the corridors of management like so many fragrant vapours. Contrary to his exemplary work ethic, however,

Dervi's personal life soon veered dangerously from decency. Maybe it was because the pay was very good; he was young and could risk dancing on a razor edge. But whatever it was, the devil got into the money and Dervi, the prodigal, sowed his wild oats. He sought to enjoy the great pleasures of the body. Material things were of little worth: he chose not to lay up riches where they would rust and moths eat them. Old friends watched him, wondering: What happened to the quiet, kind and thoughtful man we used to know? Some decided that Dervi had been possessed by a demon and they prayed for him before going to bed at night. But Bubu, whose opinion really mattered to him, was not opposed to his doings, though Dervi had to admit she did not know the full extent of his debauchery.

Bubu had studied Anthropology at the University, a little too hard, perhaps, judging from her strange ideas about society. Although she led an ascetic lifestyle, she encouraged Dervi to do as he pleased. 'Now leave religion alone; step out into the power of your Will.' This was her mantra, which Dervi finally accepted after countless arguments and made it his own.

Soon after graduation, Dervi and Bubu began dating. It was love – but of a strange sort – because later Dervi began to suspect that Bubu was really incapable of any strong emotion. She was too...sensible: their relationship was awkwardly non-sexual. He suspected that their love did not grow because it was passionless. It was only much later, after she had gone away to Namibia, that Dervi understood that Bubu might have had unresolved problems in her life.

Bubu understood Dervi very well and he found it easy to communicate his innermost feelings to her. When he told her that he loved her she smiled and kissed him lightly on the lips – too quickly perhaps, as if she was somehow ashamed. Bubu was not very expressive of her feelings. And when, standing before her one evening with a mournful expression on his face, he told her it would be better if they were just friends and not 'lovers', she just smiled sadly and said, 'Maybe that is best.'

Bubu was the only one who appreciated his dark moods – those inexplicable periods when his world seemed to grind to a halt and thoughts of despair exploded in his mind, the fragments floating away, carrying pieces of himself in different directions. He lost control of his limbs and felt disconnected from the world around him; it was as if he had become totally incapable of any sort of interaction with other people – it was like dying. These attacks of despair usually lasted less than five minutes, but subsequently Dervi would be enveloped by an interminable melancholy that drove him to drink and smoke profusely.

The attacks always occurred when he was alone, mostly when he was preparing to go to bed. They had begun in University but had been quite rare then. However, by the time he got the job, Dervi was struck about twice every month. He feared being alone because of this and whenever he felt 'the mood' coming on, he would head for the nearest bar or whores' nest. Alternatively, he would seek out Bubu – who he could talk to but not have sex with. Fortunately, these measures staved off despondency and gave him temporary freedom from anguish.

One of his Christian friends with whom he discussed the matter said to him: 'These "fits" of yours are a visitation from the Angel of Death – pray, pray fervently for your life!' But Dervi was scornful of this suggestion, because disbelief had driven the demons from his life; therefore he thought that disbelief was, at least, helpful.

Dervi's love affair with Bubu had ended as quietly as it had begun. A few months after he started work, he met a woman whose erotic strength swept him off his feet. Sandi was the very opposite of Bubu. She exuded sexuality from every pore; Dervi was quickly intoxicated and soon gave up his amorous designs on Bubu, though they remained good friends. With Sandi, Dervi found that he had hit the fast lane. He discovered a different perspective on life; one that glorified pleasure and happiness by whatever means – drugs, sex, music. He drifted into the nightclub circuit; and soon found himself spending weekends club-hopping and tirelessly changing partners. His energy seemed endless. After a weekend spent in dissipation, he would turn up at work on Monday morning, seven o'clock sharp, dressed impeccably and ready to work. He would be entirely focussed throughout the morning, taking only a coffee break and deferring lunch till late. His compatriots were used to always seeing him behind his desk, absorbed in some paperwork or tapping at the computer keyboard, his features gently illuminated by the monitor. He rarely engaged in light conversation, preferring the security of his little space.

Then one afternoon this little space collapsed.

The High Street branch had recently been refurbished; the banking hall had received a total makeover, making it one of the most elegant in the city. Bright fluorescent lights glowed incessantly from the high ceiling, casting a brilliant white hue on the modern furnishing below and reflecting dully off the olive-green marble floor to give the hall a serene ambience. It was a delightful place, kept deliciously cool by air-conditioning. A long, marble-topped counter dominated the room, separating the customers from the tellers in their glass cubicles. At the other side of the room, bank staff could be seen, busy at their desks. This arrangement was supposed to make for a friendly atmosphere; clients could see the people who worked at the bank and in line with bank policy, this also allowed customers increased access to bank staff.

As was usual for a Friday afternoon, there were a fair number of people in the banking hall – clients who wanted to complete some business before the weekend. Dervi sat at one of the desks a little way behind the counter, in full view of anyone who cared to look in that direction. He was engrossed in work and everything seemed fine until he began to mutter behind his computer, attracting the attention of a few colleagues seated close by. However, after surreptitious observation, they concluded that he seemed calm enough and left him alone. Everyone thought he was a little weird, anyway. But just as a breach in a dam might seem insignificant and yet lead rapidly to disaster, Dervi's muttering soon rose to a crescendo:

'Yea! The eyes are back! O let me be! I have done nothing!' He screamed and pushed at the desk. A couple of ring-bound folders fell to the ground, striking the polished marble floor with a loud 'clack!'

Dervi stood up, uttering a terrible groan. He glanced around with a wild look on his face and then he kicked the swivel chair, sending it spinning and crashing into an adjacent desk.

All attention had swung towards Dervi and a petrified hush descended on the room. Only the subdued rattling of automatic equipment could be heard. A number of people who craned their necks to get a better view of the action saw Dervi suddenly bend sideways as if to dodge a blow. He fell to his knees and started sobbing like a child and then crawled under the desk.

Then the initial shock passed and everyone suddenly started talking all at once. The spectacle of someone to whom they entrusted their money going bananas was alarming indeed. In the swell of concerned voices, some of Dervi's colleagues quickly removed him from the hall – they did not waste time on compassion, since the scene was damaging their corporate image. With the help of Security, they hauled him none too gently to the toilet. Dervi allowed himself to be carried off without a fight. A couple of his workmates of the charismatic evangelical persuasion were fired up and administered prayers in glossolalic frenzy to ward off what they saw as a satanic manifestation. Medical attention was also sought; professionals in white soon came for Dervi, sedated him and set him along the long road to mental recovery.

The Management of the Bank were not sympathetic to lunacy. Dervi lost his job. It had been three years since his appointment.

In those dark days, precious few of his acquaintances showed any love. It was only his family that supported him, all through the bitter months when he was holed up in the psychiatric hospital. None of his women friends were on hand; not long before, Sandi had run away under rather dubious circumstances and Bubu did not make herself available. For all Dervi could tell, she had also disappeared from the face of the earth.

About a month after Dervi left the hospital he spoke to Bubu in Windhoek and that telephone conversation marked their last time together, connected electronically across the continent.

It turned out that soon after Dervi's confinement, Bubu abandoned her PhD programme and left for Namibia to stay with her cousin. Subsequently, she had taken up a teaching appointment at a secondary school. This news was very shocking; Bubu was extremely level headed and Dervi had never seen her do anything wild or silly.

Dervi made the telephone call from his father's house. The light in the hallway was dim in a rather cosy way and the deep armchair seemed to hug him from behind. He thought fondly of Bubu as he listened to the beeps of the telephone ringing. Then, from thousands of kilometres away:

'Hello.' It was her voice, sounding a little tired or sleepy perhaps.

There was an inrush of blood to Dervi's face – his cheeks felt warm. He imagined her slender form leaning against the wall, her hair falling across her cheeks as she cradled the receiver against her shoulder.

'Hello Bubu.' He said.

'Dervi.'

The single word seemed to carry the weight of the world in it.

'Bubu, it's been ages.'

'It has, Dervi. My mother told me she had given you my number; that you would call.'

'She did it rather reluctantly,' Dervi said, recalling that he had had to plead with the woman to give him Bubu's address.

'Yes, you must have been very persistent; I had instructed that my address details should be kept strictly private.' Bubu said. 'I understand that you have now recovered from the psychiatric incident. The whole affair hurts me very much, since you are a good friend.'

She paused before continuing with an uncharacteristic lack of fluency.

'I'm sorry... I didn't think I could bear to interact with you after... that... The first time it happened, in the University, I thought it was just a one-off and that I could handle it. But this one was so serious... you were kept in the hospital... Now if we met, I'd always remember the old Dervi and I can't take it, knowing... that... that... you've changed...' Her voice petered off. Dervi wanted

99

to say, 'I've not changed! I'm still the same!' But that would not be entirely true. Instead, he broke the leaden silence with the words:

'You don't want to speak to me again.'

Bubu's reply was in a subdued voice.

'I'll not be coming back to Ghana in a long time. Sorry Dervi. It's too painful for me.'

Dervi said, 'I'm all right now, Bubu. Really. It was just . . .'

The conversation was broken by an awkward silence. Then she said, 'I'm sorry.'

The whispered words rode across the distance like a wave from the darkness of outer space.

Dervi couldn't understand the whole thing. Why would she feel so strongly about this incident, so much that she would relocate? Unbidden, tears welled up in his eyes as he asked; 'Do you love me Bubu?'

It was a meaningless and rather foolish question that he knew could not have an answer. The silence was punctuated by the subdued crackle of long-distance static. Bubu said,

'Don't you know, that some questions must not be answered.'

When she hung up, Dervi sat clutching the receiver for a long time. Memories raced through his mind in slow motion. She had made that statement before, once when they had been arguing about religion.

'Some questions are best left unanswered, even if the answer exists. That is the only way to preserve the mystery which is necessary for the existence of God.'

vi. The Strange Woman

'A man can never be too careful with women.' That was what Dervi's drunken economics tutor used to say, back in secondary school. 'They are like a bomb that encourages you to light the fuse.'

All the students laughed at the pessimistic, middle-aged alcoholic who was always late for class. He was soon fired from the school and then they used to see him wandering about in town. He died before Dervi wrote his final exam.

Dervi walked at a leisurely pace along the pavement. Each passing car made a distinct sound: there was a brand new VW saloon car purring demurely along; an old Peugeot complaining harshly along its jerky trajectory; an ancient Albion truck growling under tonnes of iron rods and spewing copious amounts of thick black smoke. A Kia SUV squealed a hasty start at the traffic lights, the intemperate driving calling forth a cacophony of horns complaining in discordant symphony.

Most of the other pedestrians seemed in a hurry, striding along and paying no heed to anyone. Their feet, competing with the rumbling car engines, made a curious 'tramp-tramp' sound.

Dervi spotted two women further ahead who, like him, did not seem in any particular hurry; other people pushed past them as well. One of the women was about five foot eight, wearing a yellow shirt and a second skin of bright blue jeans that flared out at the bottoms. The other one was a little less than five feet tall, yet her size made the lithe movement of her arms, legs and torso all the more graceful. She wore an indecently short black skirt and a ruby halter-neck top. The image was lust inspiring. Dervi thought lewd thoughts; a small fire lit up in his mind. There was a stirring in his loins. But that was not all. The short woman reminded him strongly of someone who walked the same way, dressed the same way, could she be the one? His heartbeat picked up as he hurried to the girls.

'Aha,' Dervi said, coming up behind them. 'The sight of pretty girls is all I needed to brighten my day.'

The smell of two strong perfumes wafted towards him as the women slowed down and stopped, half turning to face him.

Dervi gasped. The shorter girl looked so much like Sandi! But she showed no sign of recognising him and neither did her companion. Dervi thought it was perhaps because he had lost weight and no longer kept his hair close-cropped. Knowing that the situation had to be tactfully handled, he grinned sheepishly, while at the same time observing the girl's firm and bulbous breast elevated by a push-up bra.

'Actually,' Dervi began, unable to remove his eyes from the succulent bust, which trembled slightly as if expecting an imminent touch. 'I was wondering if you would be walking as far as the circle.'

The tall girl cocked her head, considering the situation cautiously.

'What is it to you?' asked the petite one, flicking a stray strand of braided hair over her shoulder.

Ah, Dervi thought, even the voice is equally thrilling.

'I'm going that way; I would be happy to have your company.' He said.

'What on earth for?' she asked.

'Well,' Dervi paused, ogling her lasciviously. He could not help it; his eyeballs seemed to have become connected to her body by an invisible string. The woman decided that he was some sort of a joker.

'What?' her tone was dismissive and a bit querulous. 'You better be off, minding your own business.'

'Actually, there is a reason.' Dervi sounded sincere.

'Which is?' the tall one asked calmly.

'It is because,' he replied gravely. His eyes remained on the enthralling cleavage. 'Your friend here resembles my former girlfriend paaa . . . Indeed, I could swear that she is the one.'

This took some time to sink in. The women were amazed.

'You said what?' the girl shot fiercely back at him.

'I used to f . . . '

The rest of the words were knocked away by a brutal slap. For a moment Dervi's vision blurred and his ears rang. The girl's size belied her strength; she was a firebrand.

'But it is true,' Dervi begun in a broken whisper.

'Tomorrow again,' she said, her voice taut with anger.

The girls went off, explaining to a few passers-by who had become concerned observers, that P*apa no ye kwasea paa**.

---

* This is a very foolish man.

Dervi looked around him. Three teenage boys and a girl had stopped a few meters away, watching him with bated breath, as if he was a time bomb about to go off. A few others had noticed the incident and paused in their stride, wondering what would happen next. Dervi felt it necessary to say a few words in explanation to the spectators, but he was a little confused about the whole affair and did not know how to start.

'A rather unfortunate occurrence,' he began, speaking loudly to make sure that everyone heard. 'It was a case of mistaken identity.'

Someone sniggered; there was a cautious guffaw in reply. Then the dam broke and laughter sprang up all round, everyone close by seemed to be tickled out of their senses. Why, why! Dervi cried silently, eyes misting over with tears. Dropping his gaze, he hastily pushed through the crowd. The laughter died away; but his face felt warm with embarrassment and his cheek stung from the slap. The girl had really hit him hard.

Yet Dervi had not been lying. The girl who had struck him looked just like Sandi, his sexy little ex-girlfriend. Sandi.

Everything came to his mind now, dug up from memory by the slap. They had loved each other, but she loved him more than he loved her and besides, he had other girlfriends as well. It was very complicated, but there was an explanation for all that. Sandi and Dervi used to make love without restraint. They made love to each other everywhere, even on the beach and in the bush like animals. It was hot sex.

Things came to a head one Sunday afternoon, when Sandi's kid brother found them in the garage. Dervi had visited Sandi at home and they thought that the garage, detached from the main house, offered sufficient privacy for their purposes.

Dervi had Sandi against the wall when the boy stumbled in for his bike. He stood at the door, aghast at the sight of the coupling; he did not have the good sense to leave surreptitiously, instead he cried out: 'Sandi!'

Dervi, at the height of his passion, looked around; the boy was like a midget perching in the doorway. Meanwhile, Sandi was sputtering and jerking against him – there was no stopping at that moment.

'Sandi.' The young fool said, confused and wondering what to do.

Later, reflecting on the incident, Dervi felt sad that the boy did not appreciate the opportunity for education; even more surprisingly, the chap had burst into tears.

'You will burn in Hell!' the boy screamed and fled, banging the door behind him.

'What was that?' Sandi asked, her bosom heaving as she gulped in deep breaths.

'Your brother... he spoilt everything.' Dervi said.

'My... brother?' Sandi was wide eyed. She had not seen the boy.

'Never mind,' Dervi said, patting her on the back. 'It'll pass... growing pains.'

It did not pass. The boy went hollering to their parents, yelling that Sandi was 'doing' something with some man in the garage. Father came thundering out of the house shouting, 'Where is he? Where is he?' Followed by mother tripping to keep up with the enraged man. There was such a racket that Dervi and Sandi had enough warning to slip through the gate and escape.

Sandi returned home later that afternoon. Her parents accosted her, by this time somewhat embarrassed at their initial reaction. Yet, they were still angry.

'Will he marry you?' Sandi's mother screamed.

'Yes, ma.' Sandi replied.

'Then why cheapen yourself so? Why not wait?'

'He must be very good at it,' her father chipped in sarcastically.

'Indeed he is,' Sandi admitted.

Her father beat her, slapping her about until she cried. Bruised and hurting, Sandi had only one thought: to be comforted by her boyfriend. Later that night she sneaked out of their home and headed for Dervi's apartment. She had a copy of Dervi's keys, so she could get in even if he was asleep. The closer she got to her destination the better she felt. Leaning back as the taxi sped through deserted streets, she imagined Dervi's arms around her, his words washing the hurt out of her heart.

She hurried up the steps, in her haste fumbling with the keys on the landing. But finally, the door swung open.

'Damn Daddy!' Sandi muttered, stepping into the living room. Her hand unconsciously sought the switch on the wall. But there was no need to turn the lights on. Illuminated by the flickering TV glow, Dervi was having hot sex with another woman.

Sandi fled screaming. The painful staccato cries wrenched from her lips bounced off the walls like slivers of glass and rained a blood-curdling chill on Dervi and his partner.

Sandi disappeared. The police became involved; Dervi was arrested but was cleared of involvement in the matter, which nevertheless hung like a millstone around his neck.

Many months later, Sandi's father ran out of patience. The frustration and stress caused by his daughter's disappearance had come to a head and it was time for action. He paid Dervi a visit one night.

The door to Dervi's apartment was not flimsy – on the contrary, it was a sturdy wooden affair – yet Sandi's father, a well-built karate enthusiast, broke through the door with a single well-aimed flying kick. As the sudden crash of splintering wood shattered the night like a pistol shot, Sandi's father charged into the apartment, his jaw set in angry determination and a thin line of sweat forming on his brow.

'You son of a bitch!' He shouted. His stentorian voice made the threat of violence even more terrible.

Sandi's father made one wrong turn before barging into the bedroom. Dervi, startled out of bed, stood trembling in boxer shorts halfway to the door. The older man towered over him, lips curled back in a snarl. Dervi's knees wobbled, he tried to speak, but no words came out of his parched mouth.

'You better get my daughter back to me!' Sandi's father bristled with rage at the sight of the puny-looking young man whose face, drawn in alarm, was quickly becoming wet with sweat.

'Please...' Dervi finally said, his voice a pitiful whine.

For a second it seemed Sandi's father would reconsider his intention of giving Dervi a solid beating. He lowered his fists, the frown slipped slightly.

But luck had run out for Dervi. The woman cowering behind the settee pushed against it as she clumsily pulled a cloth to cover her nakedness. Sandi's father saw her and then the game was up. The lights in the room seemed to dim as the man roared and struck out, unleashing a brutal uppercut that connected to Dervi's chin with a jarring crack.

Dervi was knocked flat onto the bed, every bone in his body rattled by the impact. Croaking, he tried to sit up, but his attacker struck again. Blood spurted from a split brow and Dervi crashed to the floor.

'Pig!' Sandi's father yelled, standing over the whimpering figure. He contemplated grinding a foot into Dervi's face, but he only spat.

For the second time that year a girl ran screaming out of Dervi's apartment and was not seen again.

The memory was unpleasant. Dervi tried to push it out of his mind by studying the pattern of the blocks in the pavement ahead, but it was just a boring lattice of rectangular pieces.

vii. Graphic Road

Despite the name, it was just an ordinary city road: a busy dual carriageway cut at a point by a railway line and passing over a smelly, sluggish, polluted body of water that used to be a small river. When Dervi got to the bridge he looked at the dirty water with the terrible pox-like bubbles and mounds of silt in it and he imagined clear waters rushing forth with a refreshing sound, dancing along with fish. He thought, most good things exist only in the mind. Dervi suspected that Graphic Road was so named because it passed before the offices of one of the national newspapers, the *Daily Graphic*.

Back in the University, Dervi had dreamt of becoming a financial journalist. He saw himself sharply dressed and speaking to the people who made the money, thereby making a bit himself. But it did not take long for reality to dawn on him. He was a poor black African. The world did not care about him and neither did the government, in whose eyes he was probably some sort of pest to be despised, unless he joined their Club and together they exploited the masses. What else was an education good for, anyway? In Bubu's words, he could either join the elite or die.

As Dervi plodded past the imposing newspaper offices, the greenish-blue glass windows glinting in the sun reminded him of an interaction he had had with a budding politician some years ago. Just out of school, unemployed and prey to despair, Dervi was particularly impressionable and found politics of great interest.

At that time, as always, the country was going through some political difficulties. No doubt, the comatose economy had a lot to do with the angry anti-government demonstration that rocked the capital city after several weeks of a tense, dramatic build-up. The immediate cause of the march was the alleged under-valuation and subsequent sale of some state-owned assets to members of the ruling party. Thousands of protesters hit the streets; skirmishes had occurred and people were hurt. The press was full of accusations and rebuttals. It was the usual stuff: a group of people wanted to challenge the Establishment.

The leader of the protests was an angry youth with political ambitions, a well-known firebrand from his days as a student leader at the University. Soon after the demonstration, things became quite hot for the organisers: members of government lashed out ferociously with unsavoury media attacks. The leader was the main target of these attacks, which were launched with such vituperative vigour that he thought it wise to go underground for a day or two. He sought refuge in Bubu's house, situated in a middle-class suburban neighbourhood; this was where Dervi met him two days after the demonstration.

Dervi usually spent weekdays at Bubu's house, arriving in the morning with a couple of novels which he read to hide the despair brought on by his chronic unemployment.

Bubu was busy preparing breakfast when he got there that morning; she hurriedly ushered him to the balcony where a smallish figure sat reading a newspaper. She did the introductions rather hastily, saying with a sweeping gesture towards the man: 'Dervi, meet my cousin, the Political Agitator.' Then she dashed off to save some omelettes from imminent incineration.

A pleasant, lazy air pervaded the scene, enhanced by the curious collection of cacti arranged on the balustrade. A little further on, a rose garden in full bloom provided a red and yellow challenge to the refreshing green of the lawn. A line of dwarf coconut trees stopped the rays of the sun from assaulting Dervi and the political agitator. They sat in cane chairs arranged around a circular table and made small talk over the morning's newspapers. The agitator looked rather trendy in a black batakari over a pair of blue jeans and his shaven bullet head glinted dully like a polished cannonball. He tossed the *Daily Graphic* aside with a supercilious air.

'Some of these fools don't understand what this is all about.' He said. 'The Government Spokesman is running gas out of his mouth again. He'd better watch it. The people are angry, couldn't he tell from the demonstration?'

'Perhaps the government is out of touch with the people,' Dervi suggested tentatively.

'Just bloody insensitive,' the agitator replied. 'They know very well what the people are suffering; that's how come they were elected to begin with!'

Bubu returned from the kitchen with a laden tray.

'Sugar?' Bubu asked, as she poured a cup of tea for Dervi.

Dervi nodded. 'Just one please.'

She dropped a single cube into his cup. Dervi reached for the cream while she turned to her other guest.

'Sugar?' Bubu asked him.

The agitator, shaking his head, said:

'Sugar...A clear metaphor for the Imperialist subjugation of the African and the low self-confidence of the black man.'

Dervi spluttered into his cup.

'Its just sugar,' Bubu said.

The agitator was not moved. The stage was set for the morning's discussion. Fifteen minutes later, the man was fully warmed up and delivering an erudite assessment of the National Woe.

'You know, the colonial masters left a system of administration designed to subjugate the natives, but upon succeeding the colonists after independence, Black governments succumbed to their base nature, which, perhaps, was not far below the surface. They did not care about the people...only about them-selves.'

Bubu chuckled. Dervi poured some more tea. He was impressed by the agitators' show of passion.

'Black governments maintained the repressive structures; even reinforced them, creating an elitist club to replace the colonialist ones. Now, as you can see, a person's only real chance of success is to join the elite. Getting a recommendation is the only way. Either you are well "connected" or you are jetsam...Flotsam.'

Bubu winked at Dervi, making him feel that the whole thing was just some kind of game. At a point in time he did indeed wonder if the agitator was just rehearsing a part as he leaned forward, holding forth confidently, fingertips pressed together.

'Many of our youth – like you, Dervi, Bubu; like me – starry-eyed, with good degrees, are wilting at the shock of this wicked socio-economic regime.

The unemployment rate is high. Nepotism takes precedence over competence in everything – from job appointments to civil administration. And now, they are selling national assets to themselves!'

'So you led the challenge,' Bubu said.

'Sure, someone had to. It was long overdue.'

'Well, I'm just thinking of those thousands of young people shouting in the heat of the sun. Certainly, their time could have been put to better use.' Bubu said.

'A demonstration is a legitimate means of protest,' Dervi cut in.

' "Legitimate" does not mean useful.' Bubu held fast. 'People were beaten with batons in the street. The Police were brutal. Did you like that?'

According to news reports, dozens of people were injured and had to be taken to hospital.

The agitator was not fazed. 'Of course not. But that just goes to show you the tyrants we are dealing with. It was supposed to be a peaceful march. There was no need for all that.'

Dervi wondered whether the man had any feelings for the injured demonstrators, sitting there in the cool mid-morning, drinking tea and discussing politics. There was something about his manner that made Dervi slightly suspicious of the agitator's sincerity. His manner seemed too smooth; besides, he seemed to overlook the individual in favour of a collective ideal. He saw only the forest and not the trees. But he was an excellent speaker.

The man stroked his chin and cleared his throat.

'In any case, I know that our message got across. We demand public accountability. We demand an investigation into the sale of State-owned enterprises. These properties belong to the nation; we cannot allow such corruption at the very core of Power. It hurts the little people! The worst thing is that this behaviour is destroying our future . . . destroying even the future of our unborn children, because apart from being corrupt, our leaders are daft. They have no imagination; their thinking is stunted by tunnel vision, they are concerned only about their creature comforts. Yet, they pretend to be great men by whose effort the country is being transformed into paradise. We can see that the truth is different. People are poor. Opportunities are tenuous. The cream of the country's educated youth flee the country in their droves, to pick up menial jobs in the West. It's the Slave Trade all over again, except that this time the slave takes up the yoke willingly; the master does not physically molest him and everyone's conscience is at peace. And always, representatives of the former slave masters, like vultures, keep drifting in and out of here, patting their obedient servants on the head. Occasionally our leaders are invited over to sup with the Masters in the West. Every dog has its day.' The agitator sounded bitter.

'One can only wonder what Kwame Nkrumah would say if he could see what his beloved Ghana has become.' Bubu chuckled, adding, 'The tyranny of the future.'

The agitator shook his head and flung open his arms. 'Despondency reigns within the country,' he continued, his voice picking up a note of anguish as he delivered a rapid-fire staccato. 'People live their lives in pursuit of money and pleasure. It is like a playground where children hide needles in their sleeves and prick each other to get access to the seesaw. And it is not right.' Then he paused, arms suspended in mid air. The *batakari* hung straight from his shoulders. Dervi was leaning forward, slave to the erudite flow of words, holding his breath with his gaze frozen on the motionless arms spread out like the Redeemer's without the cross. The climax was gentle, but no less a show of mastery. The agitator said softly; 'We need a radical change.'

Dervi sighed, relief rolling over him as the outstretched arms dropped. The man reached for his cup of tea, leaned back in the chair and took a sip. Perspiration peppered his forehead, but he appeared to be happy with himself. Then Bubu laughed and applauded; the mocking clap-clap-clap sounded hollow. She was deriding the man's great speech. Dervi was not impressed by her attitude.

Later, when the political agitator had gone away, she floated her flowery thoughts through Dervi's mind. The World was going through a Phase. Like her, Dervi could be detached and watch what would come to pass, or he could get in there and go with the flow. He would fail if he tried to change the system, she said. The forces at work were cosmic, no less. An individual, puny, would be crushed if he stood against the world civilisation as it entered a new stage. She believed that a new morality was evolving; there was going to be a new society, with new rules, different interests and different roles for the individual. Finally, the real brave new age was dawning.

Dervi was not convinced by Bubu's philosophising. She came from a rich family and could afford to study anthropology and be detached. However, though his family was reasonably well to do, he could not expect any monetary support after graduation. For him, to be 'detached' meant to 'starve.' He had to go into the field and work.

'Don't let the world depress you then,' Bubu warned. 'Don't let the system drive you to distraction. Do not be weak; take what you want without pity. Even if the World frowns at you, go forward and face the challenge fearlessly. With this you can only win, because that is the attitude for these times.'

It did not take much longer for Dervi to fully appreciate the views espoused by the agitator and confirmed by Bubu. It was clear for all who wished to see: the system was built for the elite to rape the masses; that was the way things worked in the country. A man had to get on top of everyone else otherwise he would be the one taken advantage of. It was initially unpleasant to realise this, but in the end, Dervi knew that he would rather be the hammer than the nail. So he took Bubu's advice and for a time her formula seemed to work. But there was one dark element, Dervi's nemesis, whose effect she could not predict.

viii. Mephistopheles

Dervi was first introduced to Mephistopheles when he was a child. The demon was presented to him in all his terror; his aunt Suzi even drew a picture for him. Mephisto was red all over, his skin gleamed like a stretched leather garment and a pair of short horns sprouted from a shiny bald head. Snake-yellow eyes, deeply recessed within bony sockets, glared behind thick black eyebrows; a curved nose presided over thin lips that heralded a prominent chin on which sprouted a short, pointed beard. Large hands and long fingers were crowned with sharp talons; there were goat hooves instead of feet and finally, Mephisto sported a tail that whipped back and forth. There were no pretensions in the introduction. Mephisto was going to 'get him' if he did not do as he was told. Mephisto was not kind; he would not spare a child either. But Mephisto remained tame and did not bother Dervi for many years after their first meeting. Yet the evil spirit was only biding his time, because later, he came after Dervi in pitiless attack, night after night.

Dervi spent the sixth year of his life staying with his aunt Suzi, who at that time was living in a lovely bungalow in Tesano. This was because his parents were fighting all the time and it was thought best to remove the child from the battlefield. Yet, Suzi had no time for him. She did not really want to care for a child. The task was foisted on her despite her protests. Sometimes she left Dervi alone in the house, going off to spend the evening with her ex-pat boyfriend, Otta, since they did not live together. The arrangement was quite unusual because Suzi's house actually belonged to Otta. At other times, the man came to spend the weekend and then she did not take good care of Dervi, feeding him only when she cared to.

Suzi had been an immoral person. Since she was able to hide this fact from most people, she was a hypocrite as well. She made claims to Christianity, but in later years, just before she was killed, the pretence became too intense to maintain and her true colours showed. But at that time it was too late.

She was an artist and spent most of her time pottering about the porch with paints and brushes, daubing colours on canvas, silent before the easel. Otta claimed to be a sailor on early retirement and had relocated to Ghana on account of 'the sun'. Whatever Otta had been, he was now a drug user as well; it was likely that he was a dealer too. The man made no pretensions to decency. He was bad: looked it, smelt it, acted it and didn't give a hoot about other people's opinions. A dark-haired, swarthy fellow with a blue dragon tattooed on his right arm, Otta had blackened teeth and always smelt of something unpleasant – usually cigarette smoke, but sometimes he stank of sweat, garlic and occasionally urine which leaked into his clothes. A peculiar musty odour hung about him.

At first glance, Suzi and Otta cut a very unlikely pair. Suzi's looks were rather homely; she could not be mistaken for a high-flying woman of the world. Plump, somewhat withdrawn in company and coming across as rather shy at a first meeting, it stretched the imagination to believe that she was the regular consort of Otta. She seemed more like someone's favourite aunt, the kind who invited children to her house for Sunday lunch while fussing over their behaviour in Church that morning. However, this was not the case. Suzi was mean and abusive; she also used cocaine and smoked marijuana, mostly when Otta was around. They both loved music. There was a huge hi-fi system in Suzi's bedroom, with tremendous speakers with a formidable bass output, which when played at full blast, made the walls tremble and windowpanes rattle.

Such was the company Dervi was plunged into for a year. Things were made worse because he had changed schools and lost his old playmates.

One afternoon Suzi picked Dervi up from school and brought him home to a cold lunch of rice and beans, after which she gave Dervi a large box of coloured wooden bricks to keep him occupied. He busied himself building a castle on the living room carpet.

Otta arrived soon after; perhaps Suzi had been expecting him. But there was disquiet in the air. Something was wrong. Suzi and Otta stood outside on the porch and Dervi became vaguely aware of an argument brewing. The man was saying harsh things in an angry voice. Then Dervi's architectural enterprise was rudely interrupted and the serene atmosphere shattered by Otta's unpleasant yell:

'Give it here!'

Otta and Suzi entered the living room. She was stepping backwards cautiously, away from an angry Otta bearing forward menacingly. She had a battered paper bag in her left hand and carefully in her right a stainless steel spatula loaded with white dust. Suzi's back came against one of the armchairs. Otta glowered at her. Slowly, she stretched forth the spatula as if in offering. But her hand was wavering, the spatula dropped from her fingers onto Otta's left arm and struck the floor with a sharp ring that seemed to herald doom. The man's eyes narrowed in rage. Sucking in breath, he swung his right hand, connecting with a sharp backhand against her cheek. Suzi's head jerked back.

'That'll teach you to cheat on me,' Otta growled. The white powder had spilt on his sleeve and he began snuffling it up, like a dog. Finally he noticed Dervi, who shivering on the settee, was trying to disappear.

'Hey!' Otta called out to him, as if he was far away. 'Little boy! I like you. You know this devil woman tried to mess with me, anybody messes with me gets hit and now she knows that. Never respect a woman, that's what I say. Gets into their heads. Bitches!'

All this while Suzi stood stonily in front of Otta, clutching the paper bag in her hand. Suddenly the man reached forward and in a swift move ripped open Suzi's blouse. The buttons popped in quick succession. Then he grabbed Suzi's breasts, which had sprung forth freely. Otta placed his lips on one of them, sucking at the nipple. Suzi gasped sharply. Otta turned to Dervi.

'Get out of here,' he snarled.

Dervi scampered off, his foot striking the castle he was building and bringing it down with a clatter. He hid in the bathroom. There was a dripping tap in the tub. For some reason this caught and held his attention; the drops of water falling leisurely onto the ceramic and making a

120

funny plop, plop sound, while throughout the rest of the house he could hear no other sound at all. He stayed there, wondering what was going on between his aunt and her man. About an hour later someone turned on the stereo. The shrill blast of punk rock heralded a return to normalcy. Dervi crept back to the living room. Otta had left; Suzi was in the bedroom. Dervi ate some cookies for supper before he went to his room.

Suzi came to him in the night. Dervi had left the light on; the shaded yellow glow from the ceiling lamp cast a comfortable aura around the bed. But when Suzi came in she flipped the switch, plunging the room into darkness. Startled, Dervi uttered a small cry. His eyes soon adjusted to the darkness and he saw Suzi silhouetted in the doorway, against the faint light from the corridor.

'Do you know Mephistopheles?' she growled.

Dervi shrank under the covers.

'I know you are not asleep,' Suzi said, walking up to the bed.

She was carrying a flashlight, which she shone into his eyes. Dervi squinted.

'Mephistopheles is the Devil's servant. Satan's man. And he's going to get you if you tell anybody what happened in this house today.'

Her voice was cold and menacing.

Dervi kept quiet.

'Do you know him?' his aunt demanded.

'Please,' Dervi said.

Suzi unfurled a white A3 sheet with a drawing on it. She turned the torch beam onto the picture and in the brilliance of the circle of light, Mephisto grinned evilly at Dervi. Suzi's talents showed easily: it was a fine bit of work. The fiend seemed ready to leap off the page. His red body was like blood oozing from the paper.

'This is Mephisto. He'll get you, if you are not good. You must promise not to tell any one. Do you promise?'

Though Suzi uttered these words in an undertone, her voice had a cold and diabolical edge. Dervi shivered and clutched at the bedclothes. He shut his eyes.

'Promise! Look at Mephisto and promise!' Suzi screamed.

Dervi burst into tears, but Suzi was relentless until he promised never, ever to tell.

'You know what will happen if you tell,' Suzi said meanly. 'You can see that Mephisto hates children.'

That night Dervi had a bad dream, featuring the Fiend from Hell. But he told no one about it. The rest of Dervi's stay with Suzi was filled with terror of the drawing, which she used liberally to control the little boy, with such success that she was first astonished, then pleased.

After a year Dervi's parents resolved their disagreements and he returned to stay with them. Yet, it was an awkwardly patched marriage that looked headed for divorce or crises. Neither happened, though. In the course of time his parents seemed to have become inseparable, even going on to have two more children.

Ten years later, Dervi was in secondary school. It was a boys' school and he was in the 'boarding house', along with six hundred other teenagers. Quiet, intelligent and rather withdrawn, Dervi had no particularly outstanding characteristics. He fitted well into the environment and lead a rather unexciting student's life – at least until that day in the library when, as usual, he picked up the day's newspapers. There was a story on the front page of *The Ghanaian Times*, along with a picture of his aunt Suzi and her boyfriend Otta, who was actually smiling in that shot. The night before, an unknown person had broken into their house and at point blank range blasted Suzi and Otta to eternity. Lili, their thirteen-year-old daughter, apparently slept unharmed through the incident.

The news terrified Dervi. He dropped the newspaper, went to the dormitory and did not speak to anyone about the matter.

His parents did not come to see him until a week later and Dervi did not make any effort get in touch either.

It was a sad and frightening time for Dervi. No one helped him through the initial shock and confusion that assailed him after reading about the disaster. Perhaps, his family did not know that he had read the newspaper, or they thought that it was not a very important matter. But it was important, because that night, Mephistopheles paid Dervi the first of many visits. The demon rode into his dreams on a lightning bolt, crashing from the skies into his mind and then standing wordlessly before Dervi. Mephisto just stared at Dervi, eyes burning fiercely and occasionally grinning so that a mouthful of pointed fangs flashed out of the vermilion maw. Dervi cried out in his sleep: 'Stay away from me!' But Satan's man did not care for Dervi's orders.

When they finally came to see him, it was clear that his parents did not think that news of the murder would have any impact on Dervi. They told him about the shooting, but there was nothing new. It was as if they had just read the newspaper and were repeating the report to him. The police were investigating, his father said. Everything was all right, otherwise. Was he OK? His mother asked. Dervi said; Yes.

In the week that followed his parents' visit, Dervi was tormented. Mephisto's eyes burned through the night, night after night: the eyes, the grin. Dervi could not escape; anytime he tried to sleep the terror came back again. Then one night, he was overwhelmed and leaving the dormitory, fled groggily into the darkness. He stumbled around for a little while, unsure of what to do. But Mephisto became bold. Leaving the world of dreams he appeared in front of Dervi and laughed pitilessly in a thin voice that hissed through the cold wind, the diabolical eyes shooting sickly yellow beams of light. Desperation drove Dervi into the chapel. Though unoccupied at that time, the chapel was brightly lit as always and the doors were kept open by school policy.

Dervi found reprieve in this sanctuary. In the morning he was found curled up behind the altar, fast asleep.

This incident caused a stir in the normally tranquil school atmosphere. The school chaplain, who also served as student's counsellor, spent an hour listening patiently to Dervi. Then he sent Dervi packing home with a letter to his parents recommending professional psychological counselling.

Dervi duly did time with a kindly psychologist who seemed to understand everything but seemed incapable of doing anything to banish the demon. Amongst the other remedies offered to Dervi was a return to the strict Catholic Faith: he was indoctrinated until he felt just fine. Armed with rosaries and scapulars, Dervi scared Mephisto off till the fiend became only a small shadow hiding within inaccessible recesses in his mind.

However, once more, Mephisto was only waiting. He struck again when Dervi was in University, appearing this time with such diabolical strength that Dervi fled God and the Devil altogether.

The Second Coming of Mephistopheles was as unexpected as it was savage. It occurred on the University campus, at about 1.30 a.m. Dervi had been to study in the main library, which was rather far from his Hall. On the way back he used a short cut, passing through a poorly lit section of the road. The night was unusually cool and save for the occasional distant rumble of a truck, everything was still. Dervi clutched his books to his chest and hurried along, looking forward to settling into bed with a mug of warm cocoa.

It was not entirely unusual to find couples necking in the darkness, but Dervi was shocked when he saw a man chasing a woman under the mahogany trees a little way off the road. The man caught up after a few paces, grabbed her shoulder and forced her to turn around. His savage whisper was met by her frightened whimper.

Dervi was unsure of what to do. The lighting was poor – only the weak moonlight and rays from distant street lamps provided illumination. He could not see their faces clearly because the gloom was accentuated by the dense foliage of the trees.

Then the man slapped the woman on her backside, twice, viciously.

'Hey!' Dervi cried.

They paused, turned towards him. Dervi approached them cautiously. The woman was sobbing.

'What's going on here?' he demanded, trying to keep his voice from shaking.

'It's all right,' the woman said, apparently fighting back tears. 'There's no trouble at all. Go away.'

'You sure about this?' Dervi was hesitant.

'The devil she is!' the man roared. 'She bloody well said so, huh? Just get gone . . . you . . . piece of rubbish!'

The cogs of Dervi's memory spun wildly, trying to pick out a similar event from the past. The resonance was strong. He shuddered as a momentary blackout cut out his vision. Something bad was happening to him.

The man and woman were kissing. Then slowly, a large, reddish form materialised behind the couple and Dervi heard a thin, cruel laugh piping through the darkness.

He dropped his books and stepped backwards. There was a dull thud of hooves striking the ground.

'No . . .' Dervi muttered.

The couple were caressing each other. The woman was moaning. It was a kind of sexual game – some elaborate foreplay. But it had brought Mephisto back.

A splash of red light cut across his vision like a spray of

blood against a windowpane. Dervi screamed, turned and ran...but promptly tripped over a root and knocked himself out cold against the edge of a concrete drain.

Dervi came to in the hospital. The couple had interrupted lovemaking and called for help; an ambulance was readily available at that time and Dervi was quickly whisked into emergency care. It was a bad crack; he needed several stitches and about a week in bed, because he felt dizzy standing up.

Dervi spent the next week at home, recuperating. But his nights were filled with a fear of Mephistopheles.

Bubu spent each night in an armchair beside his bed. Dervi went to sleep holding her hand and whenever the terror of his nightmares overwhelmed him, the sight of his friend was reassuring.

At this time it seemed that Bubu was more helpful to him than religion had been. It was a time of intense mental struggle; he battled with the feeling that God had somehow set him up and let him down badly. Some of his friends came by, arguing the case for Christianity and presenting a wide array of cases to show why Dervi had to persist in the faith even in the face of adversity. But this only weakened his resolve: if there were so many troubles in the world, if even following Christ was a battle all the way, what then was the point? 'Heaven,' they replied. 'To be with God in the hereafter is the ultimate aim. Whatever happens in this life is of little import.' Yet, this life determined where one ended up, in Heaven or in Hell. Moreover, people's lives were so unequal, so experientially unbalanced, so opportunistically unfair, that the question of freedom of choice was suspect. A man walked the path he did because of a million sources of coercion – overt, covert – life was the great manipulator. Could one compare the life of a little girl born in a poverty-ridden village to a child of elite parents in Accra, ensconced in bourgeois comforts from birth? It seemed that the trajectory of their lives could be predicted. 'God has taken care of everything,' his friends replied. 'And the crack on my head?' Dervi asked. But they thought he was making light of the entire matter.

Dervi's family and Bubu did not join in these discussions, being more concerned that he made a full recovery.

In the end it was Bubu's many arguments, made long before this incident, which persuaded Dervi to cast off his Faith. His new religious orientation was somewhere between atheist and agnostic. This seemed to do the trick; Mephisto disappeared again, but only for a while – until the incident in the bank. Since then, the demon had been Dervi's constant tormentor, forcing Dervi to submit to the ministrations of Polduous, PhD.

'Has it helped me?' Dervi wondered as he plodded along. 'This flirtation with the Apostles of the Mind? Everyone says that it has; that insanity has been staved off and my life rescued.'

There was a sudden shout; Dervi snapped out of the reverie just in time to get out of the way of a man in full flight, bulky muscles rippling under a sweat-stained singlet. Two other men were in hot pursuit. They were dressed in grease-stained blue overalls; one of them clutched a blackened wrench in his right hand.

The fleeing man sent an old lady staggering to the ground before leaping into the oncoming traffic and darting across the road, raising the raucous blast of car horns and squealing tyres as a car swerved sharply, scraping the pavement. It was a dangerous move; he only just made it. His pursuers were not so lucky. Speeding cars blocked their attempt to cross the road. The men stopped close to Dervi, panting heavily and staring angrily as their prey disappeared into an alley at the other side.

One of them spat. 'E ran again! I swear, I get that brother... I go kill am!'

The other merely gnashed his teeth.

Dervi sighed. After the incident with the Sandi look-alike, he had kept his eyes on the ground as he walked, hoping to stay out of trouble that way. But here, he had almost been run over. What if one of those men had been carrying a gun? What if shots had been fired? What if a bullet had been misdirected? An innocent person could be killed for nothing.

Long ago he had heard someone say that Psychology was the Science of Rescue. But rescue from what, exactly?

He mused: 'And from Polduous have I come and to Polduous will I go again.'

ix. St. John The Evangelist

The sun, lowering towards the western horizon, now flooded its rays directly into Dervi's tired face. It was becoming a nuisance; he cursed his weakness in not retrieving the sunglasses. He wiped off the streams of sweat irrigating his face, squeezing the soggy handkerchief into a little ball and resisting the urge to scratch his scalp, which had begun to itch. It would look bad in public and besides, it would mess up his hairstyle.

'Dandruff,' he thought.

A short distance ahead, a crooked neem tree had somehow survived in the city landscape and, as if to revel in the tree's triumph, someone had placed a bench in its shade. A young man was sitting there, staring vacuously at the passing traffic with a bemused look on his face. Dervi approached him.

'May I join you here?' he asked.

'No problem,' the man replied.

'Thank you,' said Dervi, sighing gratefully as he sat down. The roar of traffic had become less irritating.

He touched his cheek. It still felt tender from the slap. He was hungry, but there was no need to hurry home on account of that, since he had given away his supper to the girl outside the hospital. But it was the last day of the month to-morrow. His family would visit, bringing him a stock of food rations and some money carefully calculated to last exactly thirty days. The routine was quite well established. His sister would enquire about his health. He would reply, 'I am better; the medication was actually a very good idea.' Then they would chat: mother, father, sister and brother, but painful thoughts would cloud the atmosphere like a bad smell; sadness would creep up and kill the conversation. None of them could hide from their terrible disappointment in Dervi: a rising star faltering on the ascent, crashing into lunacy.

These visits barely lasted an hour. Dervi knew that what pushed his family out was the disappointment and pain, because, all things considered, he thought that they did quite well. He had it much better than most people with his affliction, those countless others with psychiatric difficulties who were abandoned by their families and left to eke out what bitter living they could in the streets. Clothed in filthy rags, begging, scrounging for food and loose change, they were a rather common sight in the city. Dervi was fortunate: even though his family insisted that he stay away from them, they catered for his upkeep and visited him once a month.

The other man had been observing Dervi surreptitiously. Finally convinced that Dervi had settled down, he cleared his throat noisily. Dervi turned to look at him and as if on cue, the man rose to his feet and bowed.

'My brother,' he said, flashing a perfect set of teeth. 'May I share the word of God with you.'

Dervi was alarmed.

'No,' he said. 'I am merely resting here a while. I shall go away soon.'

'Why,' the other returned coolly, quite unruffled by the rebuff. 'Are you not a Christian? Then let me tell you the greatest news of all.'

'I beg you,' Dervi said.

The man did not relent.

'God, the Creator of the World, has saved us from all pain and trouble. God has offered peace and happiness to the human race.'

'Thank you.' Dervi replied humbly.

'To every single one of us, God has shown his love. There is peace and joy, security and prosperity, love and fellowship. Man can now interact freely with God.' He said.

Dervi observed the man with a mild feeling of horror. He was young, perhaps eighteen or nineteen years old and wore a bright green short-sleeved shirt neatly tucked into a pair of tight blue trousers. His black boots were highly polished and gleamed with supernatural strength. There was a red Bible in his right hand and he reminded Dervi, strangely enough, of a hypodermic needle.

'I am an evangelist,' he said. 'I am happy to declare the goodness of the Lord and the way of Freedom to all creation! There is no more condemnation; Jesus Christ has paid the entire price.'

Dervi said nothing. A light aircraft flew directly overhead, filling the air with a sonorous drone. The man continued, 'We all need the guidance of God. The future is uncertain. Anything could happen, a man could die – there is much fear. See that aeroplane? It could fall out of the sky as we speak.'

They both looked up. The 'plane made its way slowly across the sky.

'Nothing will happen to it.' Dervi observed.

The two men watched the little white object until it disappeared into the distance.

'You see,' Dervi said.

They exchanged glances. The evangelist dusted his shirt front impatiently.

Dervi said, 'In five minutes I should have finished my rest and I will be on my way. Then, you can continue speaking.'

'But I am speaking to you!' The man was agitated; his voice was almost a shriek. 'God has sent me to speak to you!'

'Really, you are not saying anything that I do not know.' Dervi replied.

A gleam sprang into the young man's eyes.

'Oh, I see! Have you then fallen away from the faith? Yet still, the love of God is sufficient, only believe!'

'Believe?' Dervi asked cautiously.

'Yes. Do you not believe in God?'

'God does not believe in me,' Dervi muttered bitterly.

'That cannot be the case,' the Evangelist said slowly, as he considered the unusual challenge Dervi was posing to his ministration.

'In any case, God has died!' Dervi declared. 'Do you not know that?'

Dervi knew that God had not died. Nietzsche had written that and Nietzsche rather had died. Yet still, the words easily sprang to his lips. The Evangelist was appalled and in a moment of silence, looked at Dervi in shock. Then he said robustly:

'You blaspheme! Oh, my friend, what has driven you to this depth of hatred and sadness? Can you not see that the Hand of the Lord is reaching out to you?'

'The Hand of the Lord carries a hammer,' Dervi countered.

133

The Evangelist must have thought he was speaking about a judge's gavel.

'No, not to judge you, but to save you! Yet and here the plaintive note in the Evangelist's voice disappeared and he spoke with authority. 'If you reject the Lord today and continue in sin, He will judge you, He will condemn you to Hell!'

'Thank you,' Dervi said amiably. 'Now I understand everything.'

The Evangelist was confused.

'What do you mean?' he asked.

Dervi smiled bitterly, turning away from the man – he hoped the gesture would show that he did not wish to continue with the interaction.

But as the Evangelist fell away from view, Dervi's vision blurred: colours merged and the busy Graphic Road faded out of sight. Then suddenly, Dervi was in a landscape of absolutely electric construct; the colours were so painfully sharp that they seemed ready to break into sparks.

It was a kind of desert. All around him, steel grey sand stretched into the distance; the sky was a brilliant, piercing blue; the sun a stark amber blob that looked as if it had been painted by a child learning how to draw. Dervi was standing before a shiny metal ladder that extended all the way up into the heavens. He could not see its other end, but the foot of the ladder was just a couple of metres in front of him. There was no sign of life, no sign that there could even be life – but he only had to wait a few moments in the terrible silence. Then, with a sinking feeling, he saw a little red spot descending the ladder at terrific speed.

It was Mephistopheles. Landing with a swish, Dervi's old tormentor flung an arm across his face in careless abandon and cocked an eyebrow. The red skin glistened.

'How farest thou?' Mephisto snarled at Dervi. 'I return to walk amongst the sons of men.'

Dervi shrank from the demon, but Mephisto thrusted his goatee into his face, hooves stamping the sand as he uttered a rasping laugh. The diabolical 'Hee- hee-hee' was more than Dervi could bear. A flash of despair turned instantly into boiling rage: he grabbed Mephisto by the horns and yanked hard. As the demon staggered, Dervi pushed sideways and flung his adversary to the ground.

Mephisto was felled!

'Release my happiness, you thief!' Dervi yelled.

With a ferocious roar Mephisto shoved Dervi off and sprang up, his voice booming across the sterile landscape like a shock wave:

'Be damned to Hades!'

Dervi lay on his back looking at the hand extended towards him, the blackened talons quivering.

'You sad bastard,' he spat at Mephisto. 'You stupid fart.'

Suddenly the demon did not look so threatening again. The shiny red skin now looked like a costume that had seen better days and one of the horns had come askew. Mephistopheles' hand dropped to his side.

'I do not have your happiness with me, you fool,' he muttered.

'Who then? Who then?' Dervi asked urgently, sparing an upward glance.

'What do I care,' Mephisto asked. 'What do I care about your happiness? I have my own business to attend to.'

'But you have tormented me throughout my life!' Dervi shrieked.

'That is my business,' Mephisto replied nonchalantly. 'Stop speaking like an idiot.'

'You're an idiot yourself – a fancy dress joker!' Dervi replied angrily, raising his torso by pushing his elbows against the ground. Mephisto's goatee fell off.

Dervi scrambled to his feet. He faced his foe with clenched fists, ready to parry an attack. But Mephisto seemed to have lost all confidence, shifting his gaze here and there like a schoolboy who was unsure of why he had been summoned to the headmaster's office.

'You're just a scarecrow,' Dervi screamed at Mephisto. 'Now that we've met on your own turf, you give up!'

The fiend seemed to shrivel and the red garment withered and fell off like a moth-eaten curtain, revealing Mephisto's scrawny, lanky body. To Dervi's surprise the demon looked just like the priest he had assaulted at the cathedral. Mephisto pressed his knees together and hugged himself as though he was freezing.

'My penis is too small,' the demon said in an agonised whisper.

Dervi looked at the disappointing little widdle and roared with laughter, shattering the landscape; dissolving the vision.

Graphic Road cut into Dervi's consciousness instantly.

136

The sun blasted back, glinting off the endless line of windscreens; his ears were assaulted by growling engines and querulous horns, whiffs of diesel exhaust stung his nostrils.

The Evangelist, still standing in front of him, was alarmed at this sudden burst of mirth.

'Are you all right?' he asked, backing away from Dervi.

'Bless you,' Dervi said condescendingly. 'I am doing great.'

The bench squeaked as Dervi rose, nodding briskly at the Evangelist who stepped aside, pressing the Bible to his bosom with folded arms.

This encounter had provided the impetus to complete the trip; Dervi could not bear to remain with the needle-like soul winner. The Evangelist himself now thought it best to leave Dervi alone.

'Bold!' Dervi declared, taking on a marching stance; but soon he gave it up and lapsed into a tired slouch.

x. Suzi In The Sky With Diamonds

It was a day of great surprises. Dervi was on the last lap home and he told himself that he would brook no more distractions. He had lost his sunglasses, given away his money and now had to walk; he had been mocked by schoolgirls, slapped by a virago, evangelised by a soul winner – it was enough. Considering that he was not going to have supper, it was more than enough.

But it was not over. As he trudged along, keeping his eyes lowered to avoid trouble, he heard someone call his name. A number of people were sheltering from the sun at a bus stop to his right; one of them had stretched her hand in a cautious wave. He could not recognise her, but she seemed to know him quite well.

'Dervi?' she said again, faltering; her hand dropped and she looked embarrassed.

Dervi was trying to remember who she was. Sometimes his memory hiccuped and went off track; he would forget the name of something even when he was looking right at it. If he concentrated hard enough he would remember, but maybe not quickly enough.

This time though, after a minute of digging deep into the recesses of his memory, the answer popped into his mind and his brow relaxed in relief. The woman was Lili, his cousin. Dervi wondered what she was doing there, but then he remembered that Lili worked in one of the posh offices along Graphic Road – she was into insurance or something financial.

She would have been Suzi's spitting image, but her light skin colour declared the mixed-race parentage. Clothed in a designer suit with hair falling glossily over her collar, snub nose pinched between a trendy pair of rimless glasses, she looked every bit like a career woman on the rise.

'How are you, Lili?' Dervi asked.

'I am fine, by the grace of God. Just closed from work, got to rush home. My little boy, you know.' She replied cautiously.

Dervi acknowledged her answer with a nod and Lili smiled somewhat nervously. He wondered why Lili had mentioned her child; was it because she knew he had no children and probably would never? Dervi suspected that Lili was embarrassed to be seen speaking to him in public. He understood her, though. Suppose one of her peers came up, or saw them from a distance. How would she respond when they asked, 'Gee! Who was that weirdo you were with the other evening?' So why the hell had she called him?

Lili ... Suzi. The resemblance was so strong that Dervi grimaced at the memory of his aunt, who had been killed and was now playing sceptre games with Mephisto in the sky. Bubu was also in the sky, but Dervi was sure she would stay well away from Mephisto. Bubu had been his friend; she had even sent him a letter announcing her death.

But Lili was speaking.

'My car has broken down,' she said. 'I have to go by taxi today.'

Another unnecessary and rather foolish statement – why did she think he cared about her car? She only wanted to show her class; she was mocking him. He always felt uneasy whenever Lili was nearby, because it seemed that there were many things that were too explosive to speak about. It was like navigating a minefield of dangerous ideas, dangerous memories.

'I'm going home too,' Dervi said.

'Walking?' she asked.

'It's not far.'

'So how are you doing, Dervi? It's been a long time since we last met.' Lili said, as if she had not heard him speak.

'Oh, just the usual stuff.' Dervi replied.

She could see that he did not want to talk. This is where honest people say goodbye, she thought.

'We all have great faith in your ability,' Lili said. 'It is just a matter of time now.'

Lili's attitude now filled Dervi with mirth. Of course, she was just patronising him. Maybe she thought it would make him feel good. People always thought he saw less than they showed, when in fact he could see much more. Dervi knew that she was lying. Lili didn't care about him, so why did she bother? Closing his eyes, he raised his face to the sky and had a good laugh. When Dervi looked again, Lili was gone. He was surprised. Could he have been laughing that long? Maybe a bus had come and she'd jumped in.

xi. The Hammer of God

The memory of Bubu's death filled Dervi with a painful nostalgia. He did not care about Lili's disappearance: maybe he had only imagined it, after all. But the letter...

It was postmarked Windhoek, two months after it was written. The contents were etched into his memory.

Dervi,

I am in Johannesburg for a medical review. I came to this hospital and they have wonderful new machines with which they looked and they found a tumour. That does not necessarily mean that I am going to die, but I am going to. It is bad. I told mother to send this to you after I died. If you are reading this, then...

I trust my mother.

Dervi, once you asked me if I was happy.

No. I was not happy then, I am not happy now. But I am seeking a deeper reason for living. I can't bear to be just an ordinary fool – get an education, fit into the system, fight for comfort, be happy over trivia and die – an unnecessary life. Life must transcend individual happiness.

But I loved it when we were together, only I did not know whether you were happy with me and I couldn't begrudge you happiness. That is why I stood aside when you ran off with that girl. Even though I loved you.

I think that we are structured to desire happiness. Which means we cannot be happy (at least not all the time). Progress results because man wishes to be happy, but thinks that he is unhappy. What would society be like if all individuals were made happy by the same sort of thing? Could be Heaven. Could be Hell.

Was Christ a happy man?

Dervi. I am going to die. When you went into the mental hospital, I thought I couldn't bear to see you again. Now I can't, even if I wished to.

And I do.

Goodbye.

Bubu had sent him a message from the grave. She was dead, what could he do? He had the memories in his head; she was still alive in his thoughts.

'Well, today I must be happy,' Dervi said. 'This is a happy day.'

The sun was dying out of the sky as he approached Obetsebi Lamptey circle. In a few minutes he would be home; it would still be light, but maybe not enough to drive away the shadow of God, falling across his bed in the darkness and giving him nightmares. Yet his medication had been increased, he would feel better and happy: otherwise, what was the point of it all? Dervi wondered if Pol was also living for happiness. 'Perhaps,' he concluded. 'After all, I am the one who is ill, the one who must swallow this medicine in order to function. It's all a chemical imbalance, one must understand.'

Home appeared around the next turn. The dour, dirty orange walls made a foreboding statement in three storeys. A sudden gust of wind hurled dust across the street, sheets from a discarded newspaper fluttered into the open drain beside the road. Dervi pushed through the gates into the courtyard, gritting his teeth at the rusty squeal. He nodded in response to the greetings offered by an elderly woman on her way out, demurely dressed in a *kaba*, complete with a headscarf. Maybe she was one of his neighbours, but he could not tell for sure. He wondered where she was going – to an evening church service or perhaps to visit a friend?

It could have been the wry smile that played on her lips or her purposed, unfaltering steps that made Dervi stop and turn around. He wanted to run and grab her hand. Questions burned off his tongue; if she could answer them, he would be content. Are you happy? Do you seek happiness and if it were a commodity, how much would you give in exchange? Would you give your soul? He thought; a man kills another to guarantee his happiness, but even man's best intentions are driven by a desperate

142

search for happiness, though this is often masked. So what is happiness? Is it not enough, just to be free from pain?

Dervi stepped forward again. A melancholy air, deepening with dusk, hung over the building. Pausing before the staircase, he felt sad that the day was over. The steps led upwards into gloom. Thoughts of God came crowding into his mind.

'Christ!' He muttered. 'It is all over, or it will soon be over. Yet, the waiting is dreadful. This pantomime has to end sometime.'

He stood still, gathering strength for what lay ahead. Memories of the past surged through his mind; his life was a mistake.

'Well! There's nothing for it,' Dervi said, setting his foot on the first step.

There was a scratching sound close by, like someone scraping the sole of a shoe on the bare concrete floor. Looking around, Dervi saw a dwarfish man crouching in the shadows behind the stairs.

'What are you doing there?' Dervi demanded.

'None of your business,' the hunchback snapped in a dry, cracked voice that seemed misshapen as well.

'I live here,' Dervi said. 'It is my business.'

The other man only muttered something under his breath as he looked up at Dervi, with an impudent curl around his thick lips. His small eyes were recessed in puffy folds of flesh and the shaven head looked like an old palmwine gourd bobbing on his short neck. His nostrils flared out above his fat lips and Dervi was not amused by the resemblance to sausages.

'Who are you?' Dervi asked.

'I am the Hammer of God,' the man declared boldly, waving a fist at Dervi.

Dervi was taken aback.

'You look as though you have been hammered by God,' he observed rather mildly.

'I am the Hammer of God!' the man shouted, stepping forward menacingly. His shirt looked like a jute sack and his baggy trousers spilled over large brown shoes with square toecaps.

'Very well then,' Dervi said, in a placatory tone. 'You are the Hammer of God.' Dervi decided to ignore the man, after all it was a free country – the man could go where he pleased and say anything he wanted to. Besides, maybe he *was* the Hammer of God. But Dervi did not care about that.

As he turned away he saw the knife in the hunchback's hand: a gleaming, six-inch blade with serrated edges. The man gestured at the yawning black maw of the stairwell, instantly multiplying Dervi's dread of the darkness up there.

'Up!' The Hammer of God commanded.

The cruel point of the knife glinted like a murderous gem that had sprouted out of the man's hand.

'Up!' the man ordered again, fiercely.

Dervi's heart thudded and his mouth ran dry. Too scared to shout, he placed a rubbery hand against the wall to steady himself.

The hunchback drew closer and the grim look on his face made Dervi step backwards while the other stepped forward; so they ascended the stairs, Dervi's eyes fixed on the power in his attackers' hand.

Dervi stopped on the first landing. The hunchback looked less threatening in the grainy light and this made his fear drain away. Maybe the knife is not even real, he thought. It seemed absurd that he would come to grief this close to his domicile.

'What do you want with me?' Dervi asked.

The Hammer of God snorted.

'I doubt that I could help you,' Dervi said.

'Keep climbing!' the hunchback growled, his grating voice sounding even more sinister.

But Dervi now thought that the whole episode was rather amusing and he smiled as he continued up the stairs. It was a children's game. As darkness closed around them, Dervi stopped climbing.

'As you can see, it is very dark here. The wiring is all gone,' he said.

The only reply was the slow, measured breathing of his attacker, which carried a faint smell of garlic and stale urine. Dervi remained still, as if pinned in place by the darkness and the deep breaths, which now seemed to beat the countdown to an explosion.

It was not a game, really. He imagined the hunchback stepping forward, scything upward in one swift move: blood spurting, guts spilling out of his split abdomen. . .

Sweat broke out on Dervi's face. He had checkmated his opponent, now he waited for the next move.

The Hammer of God struck like a lightning bolt, springing forward and driving a shoulder into Dervi's belly. The pain seemed to multiply the darkness a hundredfold as he fought for breath, pawing the wall to keep his balance. The Hammer of God was merciless: he swung a fist into Dervi's groin. Pain tore through his body like a million needles and Dervi sank to the ground in silent anguish, both hands on his crotch.

'You making fun of me, huh? Huh?' the hunchback snarled.

A beam of light cut through the dark, revealing Dervi curled up and whimpering on the steps. The hunchback had stuck the knife into his belt and now brandished a flashlight, momentarily blinding Dervi with the powerful beam. Looking incredibly strong and powerful the hunchback casually reached forward and Dervi gave up the satchel without protest.

The man thrust a hand into the bag, feeling around a bit before bringing out the small plastic bottle. He grunted with surprise and shone the light onto the label, his lips moving slowly as he struggled to read the small print.

Then the flashlight beam fell directly on Dervi's face again. He shut his eyes, but the light glowed scarlet through his eyelids.

'Are you mad?' the Hammer of God asked sympathetically.

Dervi groaned in pain and pressed against the wall, keeping a wary eye on his attacker, who turned his attention to the bottle once again, unscrewing the cap and sniffing at the pills. Then he shook one pill into his mouth.

Dervi's jaw dropped in shock, but a morbid curiosity stopped him from protesting as the man popped a second and then a third pill.

'What!' said the Hammer of God, capping the bottle and tossing it aside. 'That's all I get? My first mugging and pills is all I get.'

He shone the beam into Dervi's face again, leaning forward to see better.

'How could you be so...' he paused. 'How could you be so...' The garlic on his breath smelled awful.

He seemed to be having some difficulty finding the right word.

'How could you be so sad?' the Hammer of God finally asked.

Dervi detected a note of anguish in his voice. They stared at each other silently. Then the hunchback turned and went down the stairs.

'Wait,' Dervi said, as the pool of light disappeared round the flight of steps, plunging the place into darkness. The sound of the other man's feet was the only reply: a cautious tap, tap.

'Are you happy?' Dervi shouted.

Tap, pause; tap, pause.

'Why are you the Hammer of God?' Dervi shouted again.

The words sounded hollow and the faint echo was eerie. He scrambled to his feet, of half a mind to start after the hunchback. He could no longer hear the footsteps.

Dervi felt around for the medicine bottle. It must have

been lying at the edge of a step because when his fingers made contact, it rolled down the steps with a clack, clack: a feeble imitation of the hunchback's grave footsteps.

But then, like a blast of cold air through an open door, the hunchback's voice roared upwards with an air of grim finality:

'Because this is the time to tear down what has been built!'

Chapter 9

Three Conversations with Ayuba

i. Prelude

RECENTLY, MHAN HAD become unhappy.

A salesman in an auto showroom, he lived alone, considered himself free of emotional attachments and liked it that way. In his spare time, he read classics or tended the small garden behind his house. He was content and happy to leave things just the way they were.

The changes began innocuously, with moments of despondency that descended on him every morning. He would suddenly feel a deep unease that quickly grew into a terrifying despair: there was an abyss yawning at the edge of his consciousness. Then as suddenly as it had come, the feeling would disappear and he would revert to normalcy. However, these periods of unhappiness grew longer until each day was filled with misery. His life teetered on the precipice of insanity. Medical attention was recommended, but Mhan knew that his problem was beyond the ordinary. It was a disease of the soul, a

149

problem striking at him from the Otherworld; that was where the solution would be found.

Little by little, Mhan became conscious of the existence of Ayuba, in a manner similar to the awareness of his unhappiness. It began as an idea about someone who would save him from this trouble. As time went by he understood that this man was called Ayuba. Where had the idea of Ayuba come from? Perhaps from a newspaper: Ayuba might have advertised in the national dailies – See Ayuba for the solution to all your life's problems.

Little by little, Ayuba came to represent the ultimate solution to Mhan's difficulties.

One morning, struggling awake from a nightmare at four a.m., Mhan knew that things had come to a head. Grainy half-light seeping through the window-blinds cast the woman beside him in an ethereal mould with her long hair spread untidily over the pillow. He drew away, faintly horrified by her large breasts that trembled with every breath. Mhan did not know her; they had met barely five hours before and she had agreed to spend the night with him. But that enterprise had not helped. He was still unhappy.

Despair gripped him by the throat and began to throttle him slowly. Struggling for breath, he managed to croak for help, but the woman did not stir. Alone, he fought the malevolent spirits that had come to assure him of endless unhappiness. Relief finally came to Mhan when he fell off the bed, landing with a hip-jarring thud. As he lay there, staring upwards into the gloom, he knew that his problem was now unbearable. But at that moment his mind settled on Ayuba. At last it was clear that Ayuba was his only hope.

Mhan turned the bedside lamp on and reached for the pile of old newspapers that had accumulated beside his bed. He searched for an advertisement that mentioned Ayuba, but an hour's labour revealed nothing bearing more than a vague semblance. An Indian guru offered mystical assistance; a Christian church was open for prayers and counselling; a psychiatric hotline was available for the distressed. Mhan tossed the last newspaper away with a sigh. He wanted to curl up and die.

The woman's steady breathing began to irritate him as well. How could she be so calm...!

Then it struck him. Ayuba was in the telephone directory. Mhan remembered having come across the entry long ago. At that time he had found it amusing. Now, flipping anxiously through the thin pages, he just wanted to find it. The consultancy was there all right, listed as 'I, Ayuba' in bold black letters against the yellow sheet. Mhan snatched at the telephone on the bedside table.

'Ayuba,' he whispered with fevered breath into the mouthpiece as he dialled the number.

It was five-thirty a.m. The telephone rang, over and over again and then a machine answered, saying: 'Now you need me, now you have found me. Sunday afternoon is open for consultation.'

***

151

Mhan began his quest on a beautiful Sunday afternoon. Travelling by bus, it took a little over one hour to get to the little village where Ayuba lived. It was a bright and sunny day; the clear blue skies were only occasionally marred by puffs of white clouds drifting lazily across the heavens. The air was fresh and a cool breeze lifted his spirits. For the first time in weeks Mhan became cheerful, whistling as he strode along.

Ayuba's residence was a little distance away from the village – Mhan followed a deserted side road that led due north. Thick, impenetrable foliage grew high all around and the overhanging branches of many huge trees made the road a long green tunnel. The golden blast of sunshine was soon transformed into a gentle play of light in shades of green. The forest was alive with sounds: an occasional loud squawk cut through the shrill cry of countless insects; there was a faint sound of dripping water.

The road did not change much over the next fifteen minutes and Mhan wondered why he had met no one except for the few villagers who had been loitering about the bus terminal. Certainly Ayuba would be rather busy; many would seek a man who proposed solutions to all problems.

A road intersection appeared to the east, an abrupt gap in the foliage that seemed to have been made recently. According to the directions, this was the way he was to go. Mhan stepped beyond the shade of the trees, blinking in the bright sunlight. Then he saw what lay before him and for the moment, could not move a step further.

It could only have been the work of a genie from a magic lamp: the huge expanse of parkland, endless lawns that looked like a golfers' paradise, an incredible mix of colours from rows of exotic flowers and countless shades of green from ornamental trees. The enchanting scene extended, seeming endless, to the left, to the right and ahead to the horizon. Mhan was awestruck, but what made him gape was the symmetry of the layout: everything that appeared on the left-hand side was replicated on the right. And as he watched, all the background noises faded and silence reigned: it seemed that the entire world had been stilled by supernatural command.

Mhan stepped forward onto the paved driveway. It was about ten feet wide: a bland grey gash in the lush green lawn that rolled towards distant rows of trees on either side. The road led straight ahead to a square building rising dazzling white above the sea of green and thrusting a bright red roof upwards; the simple structure made a daring statement on the eastern horizon, holding itself boldly against the stark blue of the sky.

On either side of the road there was a row of man-sized statues. Cast in bronze and set on marble pedestals, the sombre figures reared up, each striking a different posture: running, walking, kneeling, sitting and crawling. Yet, all of them had their faces turned east, towards the end of the driveway and for emphasis, each one pointed a finger at the building that stood there.

Mhan cut a frightened, lonely figure, hurrying along the driveway. He was uneasy because he seemed to be the only living being in all that great expanse, but the silence worried him most, bearing so heavily on his senses that it seemed even to dim the brightness of the sun.

As he approached, the building began to encompass all of his reality: the trees disappeared, the lawns faded away and the driveway itself seemed only an extension of the sweeping marble steps that led to the imposing mahogany doors before which he presently stood.

A golden nameplate gleamed against the dark wood of the door. It was engraved with the words, 'I, Ayuba'. Hanging menacingly above the nameplate was a huge brass knocker fashioned in the form of a fist.

With a trembling hand, Mhan lifted the knocker and let it fall. It struck the wood with a hollow boom and the sound echoed with an unnatural persistence, again and again with seemingly undiminished strength, but finally the reverberations died away. Then the door swung open noiselessly.

The bright light of the west bound sun entered the room, throwing Mhan's shadow into the gloomy hall beyond. As far as he could see, the cavernous hall was entirely bare and empty. The sunlight reached all the way to the far side, terminating at an open doorway and making a glowing pathway on the polished mahogany floor; a pathway leading inexorably towards the open door at the other side of the hall.

Mhan shivered in a sudden chill as he contemplated the empty room and his trepidation quickly grew into terror. There seemed to be a force blindly insisting that he turn and flee: this feeling was so great that he had to grip the doorpost to remain steady.

Mhan struggled against the fear, gritting his teeth and holding on to the doorpost even when his fingers began to ache. But he prevailed and entering the hall, approached the door with a slow tread and ever increasing dread. Once again his universe seemed to telescope into that single open doorway, drawing him closer and closer until he finally, passed into the room beyond.

It was a spacious but spartanly appointed office and though well lit, the room provided no reprieve from the fear and uneasiness that he had felt in the gloom of the outer hall.

The ceiling was high, in the fashion of colonial-style buildings, but it had embedded electric lamps, very much in modern taste. The polished floorboards weakly reflected the yellow glow from the ceiling lamps. Tall bookcases lined the walls; every inch of space within them was taken up by a resplendent array of meticulously arranged books. All this, added to the deep enshrouding silence, created an aura of learned authority.

Then Mhan saw the man.

It was the strangest thing, because he seemed to have materialised within the brief moment it took for Mhan to glance around. Right in the middle of the room, statuesque and with terrible majesty, the man sat behind a huge desk made from some dark wood so well polished that the bare top gleamed richly. An immaculate black coat clung to his broad shoulders, his shirt was of a fine, shimmering silk and the golden cuff links were in the form of crossed swords.

155

Sitting motionless with clasped hands resting on the desk, the man wore a deadpan look, as if he had not noticed Mhan's entry – or, indeed, as if Mhan's entry was of no significance at all.

The abominable silence seemed to radiate from him in mighty waves.

And Mhan knew that this was Ayuba.

ii. Interaction I

Ayuba's shoulders loomed solid above the desk and his skin glowed like burnished brass. The two-inch halo of black wool on his head exuded a rich lustre. With piercing eyes gleaming from beneath a thin line of eyebrows and a nose that rose sternly over a clipped moustache, Ayuba looked powerful; the kind of person Mhan would be glad to have as a companion in a dangerous alley at night. But Ayuba's thick lips were red and moist and his tongue darted out regularly from behind a row of sparkling white teeth to lick his lips. Mhan was reminded of a reptile and this made him ill at ease.

Ayuba did not smile; his welcome was terse. He gestured at the chair opposite and after Mhan sat down the two men looked gravely at each other, poker faced across the large desk.

Mhan told Ayuba everything about his problem, emphasising that the situation had become desperate. Ayuba listened in silence, sitting motionless and expressionless in the huge chair.

156

'Your case is rather unusual,' Ayuba said, when Mhan finished speaking. 'Yet, your problems can be solved. It requires a lot more perseverance, that's all.'

'So there is a way out?' Mhan asked hopefully.

'Of course there is a way out,' the other replied. 'I am Ayuba. You came to see me for the resolution to your problems, as many others see it fit to do and no one is disappointed. If you follow my instruction, you will certainly be saved.'

'This means that I have to save myself,' Mhan said, his face creasing in doubt. 'I prefer to be saved, than to save myself. I am sure it is better that way.'

Ayuba said,

'You may feel it is better that way, but I assure you it is better my way. You must find an item. Find it and take hold of it. Once it is in your hands you will experience a sudden transformation: in a burst of fire; your old self will be destroyed and you will take on a new form. Strong, fearless, understanding and much and above all, happy.'

'My problems will be solved?'

'Yes. Indeed, these problems will no longer be yours. Your new self will be superman.'

'What must I do?' Mhan asked urgently.

Ayuba leaned forward over the desk, raising clasped hands to his chin.

'You are required to find *enots a morf retaw*.* Ayuba said. 'Now you know that it is the only way that you too

* water from a stone.

can live profitably. Without it, you will be in misery all the days of your life. With it, you will escape to a glorious life. We can only hope that you find it.'

Mhan sat straight up in his chair, gripping the edge of the table. His faltering gaze met Ayuba's.

'I will find it.' He tried to sound bold.

Ayuba's gaze only seemed to become fiercer. Mhan, though wilting under the severe look, said again, this time in a loud voice:

'I will find it!'

His voice seemed to have broken some sort of spell; the room suddenly looked brighter and Ayuba leaned back in his chair. Mhan sighed, relieved.

When Ayuba spoke again his voice sounded soothing.

'With determination, you just might find it. Yet you understand that you must find it.'

Mhan nodded, looking away from Ayuba. His gaze fell on one of the bookcases and the rows of leather-bound tomes that stood resplendent on the shelves, in their muteness declaring great treasures of hidden knowledge.

If Ayuba's way failed, or if he failed, Mhan knew that he would continue to face the excruciating pain of being weary of life, a pain that was foolish in its meaninglessness. When he turned to face Ayuba again Mhan had made up his mind.

'I shall do what you say. I believe you.' He said.

'But do you trust me?' Ayuba asked.

Mhan did not know what to say. Ayuba's voice became more soothing than before.

'Your search might take some time, years perhaps.

Then again, it might not be so. You could find *enots a morf retaw* today, immediately you step out of this room.'

Mhan looked around again. The books stared back blandly.

'Show me how,' Mhan said, rather unenthusiastically. He was resigned to his fate.

Ayuba cleared his throat and gave Mhan another fierce look. With a voice heavy with authority, he said,

'You already know that your problem has roots in the Otherworld. There also lies the solution. The Otherworld exists along with this world and the two inter-penetrate. In general, mere mortals are only aware of their world. I, Ayuba, live in both worlds at once and I shall grant you the power to become aware of the Otherworld, but only to a small degree. Thus, you must not be surprised at persons appearing or disappearing, of voices and apparitions. Never think for one moment that these are unreal. They are real, though you will be the only one aware of them and those with you might think that you have lost your mind.'

***

Later on in the day, when Mhan had returned home, he found that every single detail of the morning's events stood clear in his mind. Yet it was all too fantastic – like a weird dream – and Mhan was quite confused about what had really happened. However, he took the whole affair very seriously. Ayuba had given him a detailed description of *enots a morf retaw* and after a lengthy discussion, sent him on his quest. Mhan believed that Ayuba could save him; it did not really matter whether the meeting had occurred in real life or whether Ayuba had been a spiritual apparition. Intent on following Ayuba's instruction to the letter, Mhan embarked on the search for *enots a morf retaw*.

Mhan's first journey was to the Great Wall in the Plains of Death. Long ago, the wall had been built to fend off some enemy, but the battlements had since fallen to ruin. His destination was to the extreme end of the wall, where the final watchtower stared blankly over a sheer cliff. Mhan had decided to begin his search there, because according to ancient legend, human life had originated at that very spot. What better place to seek the solution to his problem than where life itself had begun?

It was a hard and dangerous journey. Yet another war was being fought in that country, or perhaps it was just the previous war that had not quite ended. It was a land where heavily armed men were a common sight and machine gun posts were mounted in street corners. At night the distant boom of artillery and screaming fighter jets often shattered the town's uneasy slumber.

The immigration authorities were suspicious when Mhan declared his intention to visit the Great Wall in the Plains of Death; they thought that he was a spy. Locals who heard of Mhan's plans were horrified and begged him to change his mind because the route was fraught with natural dangers, in addition, ruthless gangs roamed about.

Mhan would not be dissuaded. Not surprisingly, no one

seemed interested in being his guide on the trip; many experienced guides turned him down outright and a few mentioned prices so outrageous that Mhan could not hire them. However, after more than a week of searching, his persistence paid off and he found someone who was willing to come along with him. The guide was a taciturn man called Subu. Standing tall and strong, his body was hidden in swirling black robes and his face was hidden in swirls of black cloth: only his eyes, sharp and piercing, were visible.

After many days of walking Subu and Mhan covered a great distance in the wilderness, finally reaching the ancient wall. Then they followed it as it twisted and turned, navigating a lonely path in the barren landscape. Their destination, the last crumbling outpost, was many miles away.

Despite fears that armed and lawless men would do them ill, Mhan and Subu encountered no danger except for the occasional snake and scorpions scurrying in the sand.

It was a desolate place, dry and dusty. The sun beat down, yet it was cold because of the chill wind that howled continuously through the wilderness. The ruins spread far and wide.

As they trudged on, Mhan spotted something glinting in the rough, pocked stone of the ruined battlement, which was eight feet high at that spot. He stopped and Subu beside him did likewise. Throughout the entire journey the two had not exchanged a single word. Mhan had occasionally muttered things to himself, but Subu had been as silent as the stones that littered their path.

The object glinted dully in the wall, a few inches above his head. It seemed like a golden nugget embedded in the rough masonry. Mhan reached out and touched it. It was deliciously smooth and felt quite cool. Could this be *enots a morf retaw*? Mhan's breathing quickened as he picked up a large rock and tried to remove the object. He struck out: rock met wall with a dry, cracking sound. Dirt rained down, but the object remained embedded. Mhan struck again and again, hammering the sun-baked wall ferociously. Loose chippings fell onto his clothes; he sweated profusely.

Soon his arm began to hurt, but the sight of the thing becoming revealed was greatly encouraging. He worked even more ardently, thinking; if this indeed is what I seek, no amount of labour must be spared.

All this while Subu stood beside him, silent and motionless, staring vacuously into the distance. Finally, the thing was in his sore, blistered hands. It was a diadem, made of gold and inlaid with precious stone. He held it up and grinned with pride.

'*Enots!*' he cried. 'I have found *enots!*'

Ayuba had mentioned that it would be a thing of great treasure, much to be coveted.

'The world is full of *enots.*' Subu said drily. 'Why are you so excited?'

Mhan looked at his compatriot in surprise. He had long decided that Subu had become incapable of speech.

'Because I need to find *enots a morf retaw*,' Mhan said. 'And already I have found *enots.*'

Subu replied, speaking slowly: 'The constituents

abound, but the composite may be scarce indeed. Even there in the distance I can see *retaw*.'

'Where? Where?' Mhan asked in excitement, looking around. Subu was staring at the ground. Mhan also scanned the spot but saw nothing. He became suspicious about the whole incident. Was it some kind of set-up? How did Subu know what *enots a morf retaw* looked like?

'The constituents abound, but the composite may be scarce indeed.' Subu repeated. 'You must understand that you seek the whole and not a collection of the pieces. It is easy to see that you have been speaking to Ayuba.'

'That indeed is the case,' Mhan admitted. 'But how did you know?'

'I have rescued many from the influence of Ayuba.' Subu replied. 'I am well aware of his methods.'

'That is absurd,' said Mhan. 'Ayuba is supposed to be the saviour.'

'Ayuba saves nobody,' Subu said.

'How so?' Mhan asked. 'He assured me.'

'Ayuba knows what I know and I know what Ayuba knows. Yet Ayuba will not tell the truth. I will.'

'Who needs the truth, when what we want is solutions?' Mhan countered, peeved by Subu's manner.

'You think that the truth will not serve to solve your problems?'

'Of course not. The truth is quite useless in that wise. Suppose that I am hungry and I need to eat. The truth, which is that I am hungry, will do nothing to alleviate the pain. Only food will do that. Do you understand?'

Subu considered Mhan in thoughtful silence.

'I am speaking about fundamental truths,' Subu said. 'Not trivial matters.'

'Like why am I hungry?'

'That is a simple enough question,' Subu replied. He seemed irritated. 'I mean a question like why do you want to eat?'

'Because I am hungry.' Mhan replied.

Subu did not say anything and Mhan knew that his answer was far off the mark. He suspected that Subu was getting a bad impression of his mental capabilities. Yet why should I care, Mhan thought. Who is this pretentious fool I have employed, silent throughout the journey and only here in the desert to begin speaking philosophy? Despite these thoughts Mhan said again, rather meekly: 'Because I want to live.'

Subu's nod was only slightly perceptible in the folds of his cloth.

'And why do you want to live?' he asked Mhan again. Mhan did not know how to answer.

'It was easier speaking to Ayuba,' Mhan said.

'Doubtless that was the case,' Subu said. 'It is always easy to speak to Ayuba, because Ayuba is there for you.'

'And you are not?'

Subu raised a hand impatiently, saying sternly:

'All you have is time. Then again, time is the one thing you don't have, because it is slipping through your fingers even as you stand here. Ayuba has set out to do one thing alone: to make sure that you waste your time.'

'I have to find *enots a morf retaw*,' Mhan insisted. 'I am miserable: since I became unhappy, my life has been unbearable. And if you knew so much,' he continued, aggressively drawing close to Subu, 'you would perhaps understand my problem and the straits of despair that have brought me to this. My life is in ruins! Perhaps if you knew the terror of my plight, you would help me and not mock me.'

He jabbed a finger at Subu, who did not budge.

'You may well be miserable and unhappy,' Subu replied. 'And it may be true that this thing you seek will make you happy once you find it. If you find it. You may never find it, or when you find it, it will be of no use to you because your time is up. If that happens, you would have lost twice.'

Mhan glared at Subu, but when he spoke his voice had a plaintive twang. 'You do not understand how I feel, Subu. I know that it is worth trying to find it. I will not spend all my life searching. I shall give it a time, two times and half a time and then a time, two times and half a time.'

'And if you do not find it in all these seven years?'

Mhan shrugged. 'Then I shall stop seeking.'

Subu looked pained.

'In that case, stop seeking now. If indeed you can stop it, do so now.'

'It is worth trying to find it.' Mhan insisted.

'I warn you about Ayuba. He may have asked you to find something that you already have, thus your difficulty. A door already open cannot be unlocked.'

'What does that mean?'

'If you cannot face the truth, you will accept a lie.'

'And what is the truth?'

'This is the truth: if you do not want anything, you will not need anything. Here is the path to true liberation, which everyone fears, because it is easier to be yoked than to run free. Ayuba provides many yokes.'

Mhan looked at Subu. Subu looked at Mhan.

'Goodbye,' Subu said and started off in the direction they had come.

'No!' Mhan shouted. 'Come back!'

Subu quickened his pace.

'Come back . . . you can't leave me here! I paid you . . . !' Mhan's voice cracked in despair. His shoulders had begun to hurt terribly; he was so exhausted that he could not imagine chasing after Subu. Horrified, he watched his guide disappear round a bend in the winding wall.

The bitterness of the landscape grew more intense with his isolation and the wind seemed to whistle 'A-y-u-b-a-!' in a long drawn howl. Mhan bit his lip, tasting the saltiness of dried sweat.

Certainly, Subu would not come back. Mhan ruled out going on alone: Subu was carrying most of their supplies. Besides, even the prospect of walking back alone terrified him; pursuing the journey into the unknown left him cold with fear. Maybe Subu had sinister intent and would waylay him. A marauding gang could attack, or he could be lost, wandering for days in the merciless desert.

It was over. The trip had been a failure; he was going home.

Mhan began the long walk back to the city. Barely a

hundred yards on, a feeling of anger and disgust swept over him.

'Traitor!' He cried, flinging the diadem far away, watching it glint in the sun and then disappear into a stunted shrub of thorn.

But he was not sure who was the traitor, Ayuba, Subu, the ornament, or himself.

iii. Interaction II

Mhan was sitting in the back seat of the commuter bus. It was an uncomfortable seat with worn-out upholstery; the bare metal poked through the holes. The windows were shut because it was raining and it was stuffy inside the packed bus. Mhan felt a growing claustrophobia. He wanted to open one of the windows and allow in a blast of fresh air, but he suspected that the other passengers might take offence because the rain would be blown into the bus and they would get wet. Yet, better be wet than die of suffocation, he thought.

Mhan was weary. He had had a bad day, made worse by the savage dressing down that his boss had given him at the close of work. The man had railed at Mhan, accusing him of ineptitude. He said Mhan was silly for refusing to seek help for his 'condition'; Management had been patient with him for the past three-and-a-half years because of his excellent accomplishments prior to these difficulties. Yet now, they had all had it with him: Mhan was behaving like a mule, his neurosis was affecting his work and he had better 'SHAPE UP OR SHIP OUT!'

These last words were yelled at him and they kept resounding in Mhan's head as he sat glumly in the bus, watching the rain sloshing against the glass.

The passenger seated next to him nudged him painfully and Mhan looked to see what the matter was. In the transient glare of a street lamp, he saw that it was Ayuba.

Mhan was not surprised to see Ayuba. He had been expecting to meet him, since it was today exactly a time, two times and half a time since they had first met. Yet Mhan did not feel comfortable about the other's unannounced appearance, because it was as if Ayuba had been spying on him and had chosen to surprise him by catching him napping, as it were.

This time, Ayuba's clothes were of the proletariat persuasion: he looked like any other exhausted commuter on his way home from a thankless job.

Ayuba did not pay any attention to Mhan: he flexed his broad shoulders, but continued starring straight ahead. Mhan considered the situation for a while, the languid coughing of the aged bus engine seeming to mirror his inner despair. He hoped that Ayuba would break the ice by speaking first, but the other seemed in no hurry at all. Indeed, he acted as if Mhan was not present. Mhan found this irksome, since Ayuba had first attracted his attention by nudging him.

Finally Mhan said, 'I have been unable to find *enots a morf retaw*. I have sought it strenuously, not a day has gone without a struggle to find *enots a morf retaw*. Perhaps it does not exist and I am on a fool's errand.'

Ayuba replied, 'Yet only if you are a fool, will you be sent on a fool's errand. Are you a fool?'

Mhan thought about this for some time. Then he replied, sombrely: 'No.'

Ayuba said: 'I am concerned that you have not found *enots a morf retaw*. You even have doubts as to the existence of *enots a morf retaw*. How can you doubt, when it is the only doorway you can find out of this gloom of confusion that now envelops you? This is the only way you can be happy. You have had a time, two times and half a time and yet you have wasted it all, listening to fairy tales and other foolishness when what you needed to do was to find *enots a morf retaw*. You have chosen to wallow in misery. Are you not miserable?'

Mhan had to admit that he was miserable. Ayuba nodded sadly.

'There is talk about God,' Mhan said.

'There is always talk about gods, *ha satan* and all that. It does not help.'

'That is not what I have heard.'

Ayuba gnashed his teeth in exasperation.

'I gather you have encountered Subu.' He said.

'Yes, on a walk by the Great Wall in the Plains of Death.' Mhan replied.

'Do not go to such places,' Ayuba said.

'I was looking for *enots a morf retaw*. I went to many different places.'

'Be that as it may, I encourage you to disregard Subu and all that he told you. He is a confusionist. I am a perfectionist. Besides, I am here to help you. We have a contract. I have shown you the way. Now follow it.'

Mhan replied, 'I have heard that there are other ways and that yours might not be the best way either. The times when I haven't been looking for *enots a morf retaw* I have spent thinking. I think about many things, I ask myself questions and I get answers. Of course, since I am not as knowledgeable as you are, it is certain that some of my answers are wrong. Yet I am sure that the logic is sound and that if I have erred it is only because I lack enough information. I wonder if it is not better to seek more knowledge, above all else. Perhaps if you taught me more about these things, I would be able to rise out of the clutches of ignorance...'

'Into the clutches of knowledge perhaps,' Ayuba said, speaking with the authority of a king chiding an errant vassal: 'I advise that you end this idle talk at once. You must listen to what I say, obey what I command, follow the path I point out!'

He cleared his throat and at the same time, a blast of thunder shook the heavens. Mhan could not tell whether this was a coincidence, or whether Ayuba really had such powers. Then the thunderous rumblings petered out and Ayuba continued to speak, but in a milder tone.

'There are things that will distract you. Yet be resolute and follow my instruction. If you do exactly as I say, ignoring everything else, you will find fulfilment and happiness. The problems that you brought to me will all be solved. I guarantee you this. In a single moment of infinite ecstasy you will find yourself in painless conflagration as you hold *enots a morf retaw* in your hands and your old self is destroyed. Your new, superior self will emerge phoenix-like from the flame.'

Mhan listened to Ayuba with bated breath. Ayuba seemed to be growing bigger and bigger, though it happened slowly and was not apparent from the onset. However, Mhan was squeezed against the side of the bus and soon he was almost unable to breathe. Yet he feared to complain, not only because he was afraid of Ayuba but also because he did not know how to phrase his complaint.

Ayuba might think that he wanted a way to escape from discussing the important issue that lay before them. Besides, there was some uncertainty about the matter. Maybe he was merely hallucinating and Ayuba had not changed in size at all. It was also possible that Ayuba might have no control over what was happening to him. This made the choice of words quite tricky; to speak about the matter Mhan knew he had to be delicate. While Mhan was trying to construct his complaint, Ayuba said:

'Still, you have a chance. Find it, now as though your life and not just your happiness depended upon it. Once again you have a time, two times and half a time. Perhaps that is all you will ever have.'

As he spoke, Ayuba rapidly reduced in size and disappeared ingloriously, seeming to merge with the unpleasant atmosphere in the bus.

The rain had let up. Mhan looked at the many lights slowly passing by and they held no meaning at all.

iv. Interaction III

The late afternoon sun burned dull red behind thin ribbons of cloud, seemingly trapped behind celestial prison bars; nevertheless, it shed light on the wild, desolate beach, strewn with sharp rocks that had not yet been weathered into smoother shapes. Breakers roared incessantly as they pounded the stony shoreline. In the distance, a rocky promontory jutted rudely into the sea.

Mhan stood about a dozen yards from the sea, tasting the salt spray thrown up by the breakers crashing into the shore.

A group of gulls circled in the distance, uttering blood-curdling cries and observing Mhan with a keen and evil interest. They looked bigger than any he had ever seen and when a couple of them wheeled about and came close, their screams made him cringe.

It had cost Mhan weeks of studying esoteric manuscripts and strange maps, in addition to many days of harsh journeying to find this forbidden place. He had read in the ancient texts that the waters of this beach had the power to regenerate and heal. Once in an unpredictable while, the waves became agitated and crashed onto the shore with a fevered froth; in that moment even the dead would be returned to life if they went into the water. It became clear to Mhan, after much painstaking research that this indeed was the place to find what he so strenuously sought. He had been waiting for many hours, standing with his face towards the sea, shivering in the bitter cold and wondering what to do next, when suddenly, the roar of the sea became louder, rising to a deafening boom.

The waves leapt up and broke on the shore with a sparkling froth; spray filled the air like rain.

Then Dobo rose out of the sea. He was in the form of a man, walking on the water naked and without shame. When Dobo stepped onto the beach, the gulls became silent and the pounding roar of the waves suddenly reduced to a bubbling murmur, like a rill coursing over a stony bed.

Dobo was huge; his muscles rippled as he walked. His face was mask-like and expressionless. An aura of bright, silvery light surrounded him and his right hand clutched a sinuous, writhing object of indefinite shape. It glittered and shimmered and shot out dazzling bursts of coloured light. Mhan's heart leapt; he screamed at the top of his voice as he rushed to meet Dobo:

'*ENOTS A MORF RETAW!*'

'You are quite mistaken,' Dobo said to Mhan. 'This is not *enots a morf retaw*. It only looks like *enots a morf retaw*.'

'How can that be the case?' Mhan asked. 'You know that this is why I am here.'

'I assure you that it is not really *enots a morf retaw*.' Dobo said coolly.

'But how do you know?' Mhan protested.

'Because I made it myself.'

'It may well be the real article, anyway!' Mhan cried.

'It is not the real article, I tell you. It is a fake, made by me. Obviously, you have no idea of the real *enots a morf retaw*, else you would not speak as you do. What business have you looking for something that you cannot recognise?'

'It is my only hope,' Mhan said desperately.

'You have been set to a task that is impossible to do, because the very person who gave you the task also took away the tools. This is the workings of Ayuba.'

'How do you know?'

'I have helped many who have been deceived by Ayuba. Alas, it is only by further deceit that they are saved. This is why I engage myself in making fakes. Had things turned out otherwise, I would have passed this fake to you and you would have been satisfied. Yet Subu spoke to me just before I came here and so I decided against deceiving you.'

'Why must everyone but I be deceived?' Mhan cried.

Dobo said nothing.

'If it takes deceit to be happy, why then deceive me!'

'It does not take deceit to be happy,' Dobo said.

'Then what does it take?' Mhan asked.

'It does not take anything to be happy.' Dobo said. 'Why do you think that it is necessary to be happy?'

Mhan gaped at Dobo. He found it inconceivable that such a question could be asked and was at a loss for words. Yet Dobo waited in expectation, so he finally said,

'In any case, I want to be happy.'

'Go ahead. Be happy.'

'But I can't!'

'Why not?'

'I just can't . . . be happy like that!'

174

'You deceive yourself.'

Mhan thought Dobo was playing games with him.

'Well, are you happy?' he asked Dobo.

'Happiness is of no interest to me. There are several other things I would rather do than simply be happy. Happiness seems rather unnecessary; one can do quite well without it.' Dobo replied.

'You lie!' Mhan shouted.

'I thought that you just asked to be deceived. Do you now complain?'

'You lie,' Mhan repeated, weakly.

'Perhaps everything that I say is a lie,' Dobo said.

Mhan noticed that Dobo was slowly becoming transparent. He could see the beach and the sea faintly through Dobo's body. He lunged at the thing in Dobo's hand, but the other stepped sideways and Mhan staggered past, saving himself from falling only by a heroic effort: turning the fall into a dive, he made a magnificent cartwheel and landed neatly on his feet. Then he swung round to face Dobo, his eyes wide with fear and the heart-wrenching light of a dying hope.

Dobo stood still, towering over Mhan. The thing in his hand seemed to sparkle with greater ferocity, whipping back and forth as if it was alive and held against its will.

'Do go Gentle,' Dobo said, 'Into that Good Night.'

Mhan felt insufferably pained.

He stood motionless; his mind shattered by the knowledge that he had lost something exceedingly precious. He felt time slip by relentlessly and as Dobo slowly faded away with *enots a morf retaw*, Mhan knew that this chance had also been lost.

***

It was just past midnight. A sickly-looking half-moon hung listlessly in the sky, imbuing the earth with a ghostly light. The wind whistled cheerlessly in the tree-branches.

Mhan sighed deeply. Though he had been sitting on the bench for a while, the hard unyielding stone seemed to be no warmer now than when he first sat on it. He closed his eyes meditatively and tried to work himself into a spiritual mood.

'God please forgive me, because I am only a human being.' He said and immediately received a sharp slap to the back of his head. Mhan yelped and his eyes snapped open. Ayuba was standing beside him.

'What do you think you are doing?' Ayuba asked angrily.

'Seeking the face of God!' Mhan shouted. 'You have harmed me, Ayuba, with your lies.' He bit his lip to control himself, his biceps trembling in rage. How could Ayuba be so disrespectful as to sneak up and slap him while he was praying!

Ayuba replied haughtily.

'Harmed you? How ungrateful you are! Did you not know about God when you sought me out?'

'*You* do not know anything about God.' Mhan said.

'You are mistaken, my friend. I know everything,

which is much more than you can ever imagine.' Ayuba replied. 'I gave you the best advice a man could ever give. You however insisted on following fairies.'

'You tasked me to find *enots a morf retaw* – something that did not exist, when perhaps there was no reason at all to look for it.'

'Well, did you find it?'

'I cannot tell.'

'You saw it, but you allowed Dobo to take it away again.'

'Dobo said that it was a fake.'

'Never mind what Dobo said.'

'It wasn't a fake?'

'You rejected my advice. You could have been in high transports of joy now – but look where you are instead, sitting on a mouldy gravestone in a cemetery.'

'This is a bench and we are in a park.' Mhan said, but he knew that Ayuba was right. All around he could see the ghoulish silhouettes of crumbling gravestones and his nostrils were assailed with the musty smell of decay, of leaves rotting upon the ground and unmentionable things below.

Mhan burst into tears.

'Why?' he whispered. 'What is all this about?'

Ayuba grinned demonically, his eyes seeming to flare red in the dour light. He uttered a short laugh that sounded like the grating of one rock against another.

Then he said, delivering the mockery with an imperious majesty:

'Yet do you not know, that there are questions so

beautiful, so sublime, that their aesthetic power alone requires they are not answered; because even to attempt an answer would be to sully their elegance.'

Then Ayuba ripped off his shirt and the harsh sound of tearing sent Mhan's heart pounding as he contemplated the demon's next move. But Ayuba only tugged his trousers a little way down, revealing the full rotundity of his paunch. Next, he puffed himself full of air so that his pale white belly became bloated and pulsated like an unclean thing in labour. Mhan cowered in terror, whimpering helplessly as blood began dripping from the talons of the creature before him.

Ayuba stepped forward, a snarl revealing fangs glittering in a glowing red maw. His nostrils distended and flattened against his face, while a sickly yellow light shone from his hooded eyes.

Mhan's terror was made worse by the scurrying shadows cast by clouds racing across the sky, periodically obscuring the moon.

Chapter 10

Jjork

The end is in the beginning and yet you go on.
         – Samuel Beckett, 'Endgame'.

EXALTED ABOVE MOST, Jjork dwelt in a small room buried in the heights of a massive building. Jjork, seated in a chair, behind a massive desk. People were always trying to see Jjork. They prayed, they begged, they cried; they fought, they killed, they bribed; they did all manner of things, just to see Jjork. Just to spend even the smallest period of time with Jjork.

They all thought that Jjork was The Answer.

Those who managed to meet Jjork would sit facing him across the desk and they would whisper to each other; for Jjork always spoke in whispers, seated in his little room in the massive building.

The building itself was a perfect cube and each side was the equivalent of twenty storeys. It was made of prefabricated concrete and had no windows at all. The single door was so narrow that a person could only get in by squeezing through it sideways and an obese person not at all. Though the building was of great size, there were only two rooms in it – Jjork's room and the other room. Since Jjork's room was small the other room took up all the rest of the space.

It was difficult to gain entrance to the building on account of the many thousands that sought to do the same. Also, though the throng outside the building did not know it, the door only opened by chance. The number of times that the door opened in a given period of time could be predicted, but the exact time at which each opening occurred could not.

Passing through the narrow door into the building, one was faced with a vast room, extending above the heads of the tallest people, two hundred feet high to the ceiling, which was shrouded in darkness because the lights on the ground floor could not reach those heights.

There were thousands of desks in the room. Behind each desk there was a chair and on each chair sat a Worker. The desks were cleverly arranged to form an extremely difficult maze and the path through the maze was the only way from the door to the exact middle of the room, where there was a small, circular platform. The maze was almost impossible to solve and few were able to make it through. Indeed most of the people who attempted to navigate the maze perished in the attempt, for *strait was the gate and narrow the way.*

The path through the maze was the only way to Jjork's room, which was right at the top of the building, but not on top of it. Jjork's room was on the twentieth floor, but only in a manner of speaking, because in the one hundred and ninety feet between it and the ground floor, there were no other floors, nor levels, nor partitions. So Jjork's room was actually on the first floor and it hung directly over the middle of the room below.

The Workers provided no help to the people who were in the maze; rather, they continually discouraged them. Since no one, not even the Workers, knew the solution to the maze, all who wished to see Jjork were hopelessly trapped.

Once inside the room, it was impossible to get out without seeing Jjork: the person had joined the multitude of supplicants facing the maze and the Workers, each quite capable of doing the supplicant to death.

The whole room was well ventilated by an ingenious system of pumps and filters and the interior was kept at a comfortable temperature: it was neither too warm nor too cold, but just right.

For illumination, a shaded lamp sat on each of the desks and a row of fluorescent lamps ran the entire inner perimeter of the wall, at a height of eight feet above ground. These lights were always on, for the building had no aperture through which natural light from outside could enter.

The platform in the middle of the room would have been deep in shadow because the light from the fluorescent lamps on the far-off walls could not reach that place. However, the platform was itself made of a luminous material and it glowed with an intense amber light, so that it was actually the brightest place in the whole building.

Thus the ground floor was admirably lit; in fact, it was

brilliant. Yet, looking upon the ground from above, a ring of darkness could be seen, somewhere between the brightly lit walls and the brightly lit platform and looking upwards from the ground, there appeared to be a void of impenetrable darkness. Upwards, one hundred and ninety feet above the platform, Jjork sat in his room.

Everyone below was terrified of the depth of darkness that hung over them like the shadow of doom. They rarely dared look towards the place where Jjork was, because of their fear.

Jjork, exalted above most, in his small room, seated in a chair, behind a gigantic desk.

The space between Jjork's room and the ground floor was empty: it was a void. There were no stairs in the building. How then was a person able to get into Jjork's room?

In the maze, all it took was one wrong turn and a person would never be able to get to the middle of the room and therefore would never be able to see Jjork. Yet, how could someone take a wrong turn if he could not know the right turn? Therefore for those trapped in the maze there was neither wrong nor right turn, but only the way they chose, for they could not tell which way would lead them to Jjork. Most supplicants never found the path to the platform in the middle of the room and they perished, for the maze had only one through path.

But once a person found a way through the maze, he would surely see Jjork.

There was a force field acting over the platform and once the supplicant stepped onto the platform, he was propelled steadily upward, in a helical path. Everything was arranged so that he was projected right through the fine reed curtain at the entrance to Jjork's room and deposited upright on the floor, face to face with Jjork, at last.

For the supplicant who had reached the platform and was rising towards Jjork's small room, there was relief at being free from the maze. This was short-lived, for a great fear soon gripped the supplicant, on account of the gloom into which he was rising. The further away from the ground he got, the darker it became. Upwards it was pitch black, but below he could see the cheerily lit floor with its desks and Workers and the devilish maze with hundreds of people hopelessly lost in it. The supplicant could also discern the annular shadow around the platform. The platform itself shone like a star and slowly the supplicant rose into the darkness, deeper and deeper into a darker and darker night, while below he could see a wash of iridescent white and amber light.

It was not possible to escape the force field. The supplicant was constricted as by a strait jacket and he could only be still until it was all over. There was of course the terrible feeling that it would never be over, that he would be thus constricted and propelled upward by an invisible force, on and on and on, propelled further away from the light and from other human beings, propelled forever into Stygian darkness. Yet it did not last forever: it could not, since the angular velocity of the supplicant was one revolution per second and the vertical displacement was one inch per revolution. Therefore, it took a finite time to complete the journey and then the supplicant would be in Jjork's poorly lit room and Jjork would gesture at the waiting chair. Once the supplicant was seated Jjork would lean across and whisper: 'I am Jjork. Why do you want to see me?'

Jjork's room was very small. There was scarcely enough space for the gigantic desk and the straight-backed chairs on either side of the desk. Jjork always sat on the chair facing the entrance to the room. The other chair was reserved for the supplicant.

The desktop was totally bare save for a desk lamp that burned with a dim amber glow and the room was perpetually in gloom. This heightened the air of mystery around Jjork and his guest as they both leaned towards each other over the huge desk, one half of each face in the grainy amber light and the other half in darkness.

The reed curtain at the entrance to the room was thick and not a single particle of light could escape from inside, even if the lamp had been much brighter.

Leaning over his desk, his head close to the supplicant's head, Jjork would whisper, 'I am Jjork. Why do you want to see me?'

The supplicant sat in the chair opposite Jjork who spoke in whispers so that the supplicant had to lean forward to catch his words. Thus the two would sit, leaning conspiratorially over the desk and whispering. Of course the supplicant whispered too, for who was he to speak out loud when Jjork, Jjork himself, leaned forward and whispered?

Jjork always had a little spoon in his hands. It was

made of pure gold and studded with platinum. He toyed with this spoon while speaking and throughout the meeting Jjork's gaze would shift from the little spoon in his hands to the supplicant and then back again, but most of the time his eyes were upon the supplicant: the other, lesser being, which had found The Way.

When the conversation was over, Jjork would instruct the supplicant to climb upon the desk and push at the ceiling above. A trapdoor immediately opened at the touch and Jjork would instruct the supplicant to climb out of the building. Once the supplicant had clambered onto the roof the trapdoor would shut tight again and could not be opened from outside.

There was a walkway of truly singular construct on the roof, leading to an elevator built into the side of the building. This elevator was a solid affair. The interior was padded with leather and there was a great, comfortable armchair inside and the air was perfumed by fragrances injected into the cool air streaming out of the overhead vents. The occupant was carried comfortably down, the doors opened and two steps were sufficient to put him on solid ground outside the mighty concrete building. Then the journey was ended and life could go on.

It was perilous to attempt seeing Jjork. Yet myriads struggled to see him, though these formed only a small part of the world population; most people did not seek audience with Jjork. That notwithstanding, Jjork's influence and power were felt throughout the whole world, though people did not care about Jjork in general and Jjork did not care about people in general. But people tried to see Jjork: seekers after knowledge and truth; mad artists and scientists; men oppressed and depressed; outcasts and mis-fits. They tried to see Jjork, though the attempt meant an almost certain death.

A 'tortured soul' once made it to Jjork. But why was his soul tortured? And, more importantly, who was torturing his soul? In order to avoid these difficulties, many simply described this person as 'mad'.

'Jjork,' he whispered, his tortured eyes flashing out of his tortured face in a tortured manner: the dim amber light in the room aided this tormented expression. It lit up half of his face and the tip of his nose. The other half of his face was in shadow, but the eye in that half also caught the light and glinted sharply.

'Jjork,' he whispered in a tortured voice. 'Jjork.'

Jjork did not utter a word. He leaned expectantly towards the supplicant. His manner was not encouraging, but neither was it discouraging. He was prepared to sit any length of time, waiting until the supplicant had begun speaking; until he had finished speaking. Then if he thought it fit, he would deliver the absolution. For it was always an absolution he delivered. Not for the supplicant – no, never. Never for the supplicant, though many came to confess their sins, repentant and in tears. No, the absolution was for Jjork himself. Jjork absolved himself, in response to the supplicant's petition.

This supplicant – the tortured soul – was of a fierce disposition and his eye in the shadow glowed so sharply that it seemed to emit light by itself, other than merely reflecting the weak light from Jjork's amber lamp. The tortured soul was concluding what had been an erudite philosophical presentation, speaking in a voice that was barely audible.

'…but in this logical absurdity lies the greatest, the smallest, the most abominable circle of all: if it is true then it is false, if it is false then it is true, do you see the circularity? How by taking a stance you are moved immediately to the contrary, yet at the contrary you are at once shot back to the original proposition? Do you see the circle, the infernal merry-go-round?'

The whisper was fierce. But it remained a whisper, for how could a supplicant raise his voice when Jjork himself sat silent, leaning towards the supplicant?

'I did not make the world,' Jjork said. 'I only live in it.'

Jjork said, 'I take care of myself.'

Jjork said, 'You also take care of yourself.'

Then the supplicant replied, in desperation:

'…Ah Jjork. Have mercy on me.'

And Jjork, absolving himself of the situation, said: 'I dispense neither Mercy nor Justice.'

He came to see Jjork one day who ended it all. During their conversation he snatched the platinum-studded gold spoon from Jjork's hands and whispered vehemently, 'I am liberated, Jjork. I do not fear you.'

And Jjork whispered back. 'Give my spoon back to me. It is the symbol of my authority.'

Then the lights went off in all the building and there were screams from the ground floor, for it was dark – pitch black, like Hell perhaps.

Jjork insisted, 'Give my spoon back to me.'

Jjork was neither angered nor frightened by this event. He was educated. His knowledge, already immense, was enriched. For although Jjork knew many things he did not know all things. Hence a new vista was opened unto him. It would be unfair to impute that prior to this Jjork was unaware of the existence of this vista; it would be more appropriate to say that he knew of it, but did not think it worthy of much attention. But when this event occurred, Jjork, exalted above most, examined the new situation and found in it such profound depth, simplicity and power that he was humbled and said to himself, 'Jjork, my friend.'

Now is the appointed time.

Sleepy-eyed, the man looked quietly at Jjork. As they faced each other across the desk Jjork put the question, 'I am Jjork. Why do you want to see me?'

The other answered. 'I came here seeking to understand. To find out from Jjork the understanding of all things. But now I have nothing at all to ask of you. I have been fortunate. I have made it to your room to see you, whereas countless others have not. However, I am even more fortunate, because before I got to you, my heart was satisfied and all that bothered me has been resolved.

'You see, Jjork, I was a slave to doubt. Doubt, I doubted all. Thus I was driven by an uncontrollable urge to find the truth, to get to the very essence of all physical and metaphysical matters, to understand that which concerned me and to understand that which did not concern me, for everything concerned me. I questioned all. Is there a God? What lies beyond the grave? Why is there a leaning towards wickedness in man? I battled over philosophical questions and tackled esoteric propositions.

'But in the end I accepted a philosophy that had already been established. I saw that it was futile to reject the knowledge from our predecessors. These same questions had been answered in one way or another. In fact, many answers were proffered and I suppose in my search I made the mistake of trying to establish these things for myself instead of sifting through and thoroughly examining the answers already existing and choosing the one which was most acceptable. And yet when I finally made my decision, it was to me as if *I* had been accepted by the Truth, rather than the other way round. Therefore I am confident. Confident, Jjork, do you hear? Even before you, my confidence is great.

'I have learned,' he continued, 'Bitterly, I learned bitterly, that I should have accepted this from the start. Rising through the darkness towards this place, I said to myself, "I am lucky to have left the maze." Rising up, not knowing what lay ahead except that in the end I would have audience with you, my mind was active. I was going over all my thoughts.'

He looked hard at the little spoon in Jjork's hands. It was barely perceptible in the weak light.

'I sought understanding. I learned acceptance. I now say to all and sundry, Do not. Do not offer your little finger to the devil, he'll take your hand; he'll take your soul.'

Leaning forward further still, this sleepy-eyed

whisperer said fiercely, 'I thought, "What if I died?" I know so many that have died. What would be the use of it all, the questions, the answers, my ascending to see you – what would it all mean then? But whereas before I had no answers for such questions, now I do and therefore I am free.'

The supplicant concluded his speech with confidence, saying, 'I am liberated, Jjork. I do not fear you.'

And reaching forward, this brazen man plucked the platinum-studded gold spoon out of Jjork's hands again. Jjork felt his immense powers wane, his exaltation called into question. He whispered urgently, 'Return my spoon to me!'

The sleepy-eyed supplicant did not say a word but simply stood up, swallowed the spoon and disappeared in a flash of murky light and putrid smoke. And down below all the lights dimmed and failed and night grew inside the great room, two hundred feet to one side, two hundred feet on the other side and two hundred feet high: the entire interior was plunged into absolute darkness.

The little lamp in Jjork's room also failed, but after a much grander fashion, while Jjork sat staring at his empty hands. With each passing second, the lamp lost one sixth of its brightness.

Panic and pandemonium ensued in the darkness below; voices were raised in tumult as the people sought to escape: but it was a veritable prison for all therein. Initially, they shrieked in sheer terror at the intense depth of darkness into which they had been plunged – but very quickly the futility of screaming was understood and with each second that passed one person became silent, so that in stages the room became still.

Above all this Jjork sat, staring blankly at his slowly dimming lamp, which continued to lose a sixth of its brightness every second. It thus was clear to him that whereas the noise from below would die out after a number of seconds equal to the number of people in the room, the light from his lamp would keep becoming less and less, until as it was for the sound, so would it be for the light.

When the multitude below had at last become quiet, Jjork climbed onto the desk and pushed at the trapdoor. It sprang open; he climbed out and stood on the paved walkway. Those supplicants who had had audience with him had been dispatched this way, now he himself stood upon it.

The paving stones of the walkway were each cut to a precise size and were of different shapes. First, there were pentagons one foot to a side. These were laid lengthwise vertex to vertex and therefore, base to base. The pentagons formed eight rows in all. The gaps in-between the rows of pentagons were filled with rhomboids and the remaining spaces were filled with triangles. All the slabs were laid with the utmost precision, for the least error would destroy the entire design.

Looking upon the length of the walkway, Jjork was immediately struck by the pattern made by the pentagonal paving stones, stretching in eight perfectly straight lines all the way to the elevator. At the same time, there seemed to be a little irritant at the periphery of his field of vision. Adjusting focus, it became clear that the irritant was not at the periphery, but was in fact right in the middle of his field of vision. The rhomboids then came into perspective and all at once a different level of order was observed, rhomboids in lines stretching all the way to the elevator. Other levels of order were discernible and Jjork saw what seemed like wavy sinusoidal lines and many different polygonal structures.

Jjork was struck by the overall effect of order and disorder, perfection and chaos; all blending together to form one credible, tangible walkway: the walkway leading to the elevator.

The elevator was towards the west and the sun was setting. The western horizon glowed orange, but eastwards the rest of the sky was a progressively deepening blue. A few grey puffs of cloud floated slowly across the sky. The elevator, all glistening chrome and rising seven feet above the edge of the concrete roof, stood in sharp relief against the glowing horizon – it was a portal to another world.

It was a glorious sight.

So Jjork stood and watched the sunset. He saw the elevator glinting sombrely in the mellow light and he begun to understand the perfect imperfection of the walkway. Jjork raised his head. Directly overhead, the sky was a deep, cool blue. Jjork feared that he would fall down, as he sought to peruse the depths of the expanse, but found that his eyes only met a limitless, fathomless space. And in one chilling moment Jjork faced the

Mysterium tremendum and light began to break through the dark, which hitherto he had thought was light enough.

Suddenly, a blast of sound came through the trapdoor:
'Do you seek God, Jjork and are not God yourself?'

The force of this unexpected sound made Jjork step backwards, still facing the elevator. Everybody in the room below was standing up. Those wandering in the maze stood still; the Workers stood behind their desks. They all raised their voices and as if on cue, cried out at the same time:

'Do you seek God, Jjork and are not God yourself?'

The cavernous room reverberated and the concrete edifice fairly shook. The great hollow between the ground floor and the roof seemed to amplify the sound, so that when it finally forced itself out through the little trapdoor, it was a great wave of sound:

'Do you seek God, Jjork and are not God yourself?'

And at each shout Jjork stepped backwards, further and further away from the walkway, seeking to escape the sound of several thousand voices blasting through the little square aperture three feet on each side.

'Do you seek God, Jjork and are not God yourself?'

I should use the walkway, said Jjork to himself, but he continued stepping backwards, for the sound and the question had become a barrier between him and the walkway, between him and the elevator.

'Do you seek God, Jjork and are not God yourself?'
'Yes I seek God.' said Jjork.
'No, I am not God myself.' said Jjork.

Faster and faster he stepped backward, his gaze now fixed upon the little trapdoor from which poured the sound pushing against him like a giant hand.

Yet, the extent of the roof was finite and the distance could be traversed, even walking backwards, in just so many steps.

'Do you seek God, Jjork and are not God yourself?'

Jjork took another step backwards and this time his foot did not touch any surface.

Jjork cried: 'Yes I seek God! I seek God!'

The second time it was more of a shriek.

On his way down Jjork saw the blank, featureless wall of the great building.

And the cancelling out is complete.